SUPERS: EX GODS

JAMIE HAWKE

Editors
Diane Newton
Tracey Byrnes

SUPERS: EX GODS (this book) is a work of fiction.

All of the characters, organizations, and events portrayed in this novel are either products of the author's imagination or are used fictitiously. Sometimes both.

WELCOME

Want a FREE Book? I have a fun little "Guide to Building Your Harem" from the Planet Kill world hat I will be sharing via the newsletter. Get them by signing up:

SIGN UP HERE

WARNING: This book contains gratuitous violence and sex, harems, and crazy amounts of superpowered fun. If you enjoy all that, read on! Otherwise... run like crazy.

If you'd like to keep updated on new stories,

freebies, and recommendations of other stories I admire, come check out my FaceBook page at:

https://www.facebook.com/JamieHawkeAuthor.

Thank you for reading!

All the best,

Jamie Hawke

* * *

Book Blurb:

A galaxy of ripped men, smokin' hot women, and superpowers we all wish we had. It's the stuff wet dreams are made of.

All I wanted to do was have some R&R from my time in space with the Marine Corps. My tour was done, my days fighting bad guys over once and for all...

Or so I thought. But damn was I wrong. So fucking wrong.

Imagine being told you're going to be responsible for bringing a child into the world, one who would have the power to change it all, to once and for all fight off the evil forces threatening to enslave our galaxy and that of the supers who brought the message.

That's what happened to me, and now I have to fly across a foreign galaxy and find the super women whose DNA would combine with mine to make the perfect match. We're being hunted by supervillains whose mission it is to terminate us, fighting off their minions while... well... you know. Doing what needs to be done to try and create a baby.

Don't judge me. Any Marine would've jumped at this opportunity, as crazy as it might seem. Just sit back, strap in, and enjoy the ride.

WARNING: This book contains graphic adult content, sexy ass ladies, a hot vet who brings it like it has never been broughten, and more super powers and super awesomeness than should be allowed. If any of this offends you, run. If you like it, scroll up and grab your copy today.

This is the story of the main character's brother from

Supers: Ex Heroes. It can be read first or second, either way works.

A SPICY SNEAK PEEK

"Payday," Threed said as she licked her lips, face inches from my crotch. Her mismatched eyes, one blue and one red, stared up at me as she worked to remove my pants. Her other hand was already caressing my cock through my sensation-enabled armor, so that when she accomplished her mission and then removed my boxer-briefs, my pal reported for duty, ready to go.

"Threed," she was named because of the way her eyes resembled those old school 3D glasses with the red and blue. So Threed, like Three-D, only pronounced like peed.

At first, I had found those eyes shockingly out of place. But now, staring up at me with her mismatched pupils and a hint of a smile, one hand gripping the base of my cock while she traced her lips with its tip, they only struck me as sexy as hell.

"Want more?" she said, and then she blinked, creating a copy of herself at my side—her superpower, and the real reason she was called Threed. She was able to imagine something and make a replica of it, though she could only really make three of something at any given time. It was her limit, because anything more than that and she couldn't focus enough to make them do anything, even continue to exist.

3D printing had been a thing for centuries now, but this was taking it to a whole new level.

Her replica immediately joined in, Threed moving out of the way but bringing my cock with her. When she engulfed it, I thought I was in heaven. Then her replica's tongue met my balls. My stomach muscles clenched, a tingling worked its way up from my shins to my groin, and I had to bite my lip to keep from yelping in ecstasy.

"Oh, the big D can't handle it?" Threed said teasingly, though it sounded muffled as she hadn't taken my cock out of her mouth. Before I could answer, she started stroking it while moving her head up and down, the replica giggling and flicking her tongue across my balls.

"Shit, shit, I can't," I admitted. Maybe one day, but

for now I pulled back, sighed, and grabbed Threed by the ass before hefting her up and onto the counter of our little room in the spaceship.

The walls were thick enough, and we were mid-flight, so I doubted whether the other girls would hear. Not that they cared—hell, half of them were probably listening in, touching themselves and thinking about getting their turn.

I needed to rest but couldn't think about that at the moment. Right then, I needed to bring it like it had never been broughten. So I squeezed her ass while she took my cock and guided it into her wet pussy.

It was tight, warm...home. Where I belonged. I slid in while moving my lips to hers, pressing firmly and tasting her tongue, then moved my mouth to her neck while my hand that wasn't on her ass found her breasts, and then we were moving, faster, faster... Another set of hands found my back, moving down to my ass and I jumped, startled, as a finger attempted to work its way down there.

"No, no," I said, also not ready for that. Someday, maybe? If I was drunk? A glance back showed me that Replica was pouting.

"You want me to get rid of her?" Threed asked. "Or can I...?"

I rolled my eyes, uncomfortable with what I knew she wanted to do, but I said, "Fine."

She grinned, blinked again as she wrapped her legs around me and pulled my hips toward her to get the rhythm started again.

"This is weird," I heard myself say, but it wasn't me—it was my replica, standing behind me with her replica, his cock (well, my cock) fully erect and more impressive than I'd ever realized when glancing down at myself.

"Did you…?" I asked, losing focus.

"Dear, honey, sugar," she stared at me, frustrated. "I can only make exact copies. You really *are* that big."

I glanced back, smiled, and said, "Damn."

"Stop looking at my cock, er, me," my replica said, and then we both laughed, and I turned back to focus on Threed. A second later, moans and yelps of satisfaction sounded from the other two, so I knew they were going at it. Threed was watching over my shoulder as I pushed up into her, our two bodies becoming one.

As tingles spread through my body, sweat formed on my chest as I lost any thoughts of what was going on around me. I didn't give a shit if watching a mirror of us turned her on.

Hell, it would probably turn me on too, if I could

focus on anything at the moment aside from the amazing feeling of her tight pussy. My mind only had two thoughts running through it—damn this felt good was the first. The second was the realization that this was only the beginning.

I was in for the weirdest, most amazing sex I'd ever had.

1

Payday, bitches.

It was time to collect the last of my stipend deposits from serving in the Elite Space Marines. Those of us who went special forces —Marine Force Recon, in my case—were rewarded with a spot in one of the few middle-class cities remaining on Earth. That was me, too poor for the Paradise Planets, but not desperate enough to volunteer for the Planet Kill system.

This money was destined for great things. For starters, a shot of caffeine to put in my final hours preparing for the last stage of my tests with the Interstellar Bureau of Investigation, or IBI. That would be followed by a nice meal with me and my brother. My treat, as a way of saying sorry for being gone all those years.

I figured studying at home while getting a chance to check in with my brother and see our foster parents made a lot of sense, but it was going to be a surprise. The idea of walking up to my brother's door and astonishing him like that made me all giddy as I approached the bank. It was even enough to ignore the lines of beggars to my left and the flying pods overhead, several of them occupied by security forces ready to shoot down those beggars if they tried anything.

"Thanks," the tall woman said as I held the bank door open for her, then another, "Thanks," followed, and I noticed the ten-year-old girl following her. Much like her mother, the girl exuded relative wealth (nobody was really wealthy if they lived on Earth). She had cute little pigtails, but her face was buried in a holographic screen that projected from the device on the back of her hand.

Holo tablets were only found around places like this bank—even with someone like me around, the beggars would still see that, and likely snatch it in an instant, making me wonder what her mom was doing letting her show it off like that. Sexy mom, but not so smart.

Hey, I noticed these things. It was all part of the

plan. We all have plans, right? Well, mine was to get into the IBI, ratchet up the numbers in my bank account, and then find a wife. If I was really lucky, I'd have a little girl like this one—or a boy, I wasn't picky. Having survived the Marines, I felt I had another shot at this thing called life, and I wasn't going to waste it by not having a family.

That is, if the gods had that in store for me, of course.

A glance back from the woman and she frowned, watching the way I was eyeing her, and suddenly my goodwill from holding the door for her was gone. Damn. I waited for a couple to enter, then followed after them so that I wouldn't be in line right behind the other woman.

Waiting in line at these things was usually a chance for me to run back over the questions and answers I'd been studying for my IBI tests, and I'd been about to do that when the bank door slammed open with a crash.

"Everyone shut the fuck up!" a man shouted, blaster pistol held high. He was at the entrance, strolling into the bank with purpose, eyes moving across the crowd and quickly analyzing me, then two other guys who looked to be in good shape. Either he was about to flirt, or was scanning the room for possible threats to whatever plan he had in mind. My guess was the latter.

He went for the largest of us first, aiming his blaster, not even bothering with the tellers or going for the vault. The victim's eyes went wide, a trickle of piss running down his leg. He was probably just a regular guy, going about his day trying to survive in this messed up world. He didn't deserve this and apparently had no idea how to deal with it. I'll say it now, and I'll say it again—no amount of watching people kill each other or fight on that Planet Kill program will ever prepare you for the moment when a gun is pointed at your face.

I, however, was special forces, or had been. Force Recon, always ready to lay my life down for my brothers in arms, for my country. Why should this time, here in a bank with all of these civilians and children around, be any different?

So I charged, slamming into the guy and knocking the pistol from his hand. It was only then that I saw someone I recognized, the man who had just run in from outside—my brother, Chad.

The recognition had distracted me just long enough for the criminal to recover. I thought he'd go for the gun, but instead, his eyes went all weird, at first silver and then black, or half silver and half black, it was all so confusing. Smoke rose from his fingers, and I was sure either he was high or I was, and that something very bad was about to happen.

His eyes moved from me to the girl nearby, the one with the pigtails. An image flashed before my eyes of me and a girl like this playing catch, or me teaching her how to swim, and then this son of a bitch strolling in with his fucked-up eyes and trying to hurt her.

She may not have been my daughter, but there was no way I was letting the bastard touch her.

My rage boiled up and came out in a war cry this time. My legs carried me forward, my fist pulled back and ready, even as bursts like solar flares started to shoot from his hands. Nothing in me yelled retreat. There wasn't an ounce of hesitation, only the overwhelming desire to make this guy suffer for thinking he could hurt anyone, ever.

And then I realized I was a goner. Dead meat. No matter how fast my punch flew, this guy had fucking *fire* shooting out of his hands. As much as that didn't make sense, it was there for me to see. My damn reality.

Fuck it. I didn't care, because I'd do my best.

I let loose, and in the moment of panic and dread, processed a portal opening up beside me, a woman standing there, and the criminal turning in surprise. In such moments, you rarely stop to notice a woman, but she was a sight, the sort of image that imprints itself on your mind instantly. Her metallic armor clung to her perfect body in a very revealing and complimenting way. One hand rested on a sword at her side, her eyes—the entirety of which were sky blue, stared at me like she'd found a lost pet, and her hair waved behind her as if she were in the middle of a storm. And that hair! A light purple, bordering on silver.

It was almost enough to make me forget what was happening, but the flames were still coming my way, their heat touching my skin. The fire washed over me, not affecting me other than that I could feel a dull pain, and I was back in the moment, attacking this asshole who'd tried to hurt the girl. My fist landed as he was distracted, and I knocked him onto his ass. Where my fist had connected with his chest, there was a burning circle. The woman in the portal looked at me, then to the man on the ground.

"Oh, shit," she said, eyes going wide. She grabbed him first, then turned to me, snatched me up by the collar of my shirt, and pulled us both through the portal with her. As we went, the man exploded, or seemed to, but then was right there, going through the portal with us.

"My brother—" I started, turning back to look for

him, but all I saw was his stunned expression fading as the world disappeared around me.

Instead of the bank, now tall walls of metal rose up around me. They glowed as if from a warm sunset, but from the inside. As I watched, black lines like thick veins ran down the walls, expanding, fighting off the light. All around were tall statues that glimmered like diamonds, but they too were being covered in darkness, like a shroud slowly drifting down.

Then a woman dressed in a black skinsuit appeared in the center of the room, at a spot that I saw was now surrounded by nine other men and women. Only, the woman in black turned to me and I saw she wasn't a woman at all—instead of a face, a golden faceplate stared back at me with a glowing skull within. Her outfit wasn't simply a skinsuit, either, but had spikes coming out of the forearms in a way that trailed back up along her arm, and made me never want to mess with her.

The sight of her caused me to stumble back, pulling me free from the other woman's grip, so that I fell on my ass. My mind processed cold, but was too focused on being afraid of that woman to have any other thoughts.

"It's done," the woman in black said, and knelt. One of the men lifted his hands and energy flew from the woman, flooding the others nearby, and then they were pulled back into their statues, vanishing with a burst of white and blue light that pushed back the darkness.

Finally, the woman in black collapsed, only there wasn't anything left of her—just a black outfit, crumpled on the floor, and the glass that had held the skull. As it smashed on the ground, shattering across the floor in sparkling shards of light, it became clear the skull was gone too.

"Who the fuck is that?" a man shouted, stepping over from behind. He came from the direction of a strange looking craft—a spaceship, no doubt, but it had the look of a missile with turrets and razor-like wings.

He approached us, having only just then noticed we were there. His glare focused on the criminal on the ground, not giving me a second glance. The criminal was still alive, apparently, and the fiery circle I'd left on his chest was smoldering. Nothing deadly.

"Eclypse," the woman who'd taken me said. "Apparently, Ranger's already sending his supers to Earth. He's made it through."

The man shook his head, gestured to the glowing statues, and said, "Our sacrifice will hold him off. We'll find our heroes to reinstate the Elders, you…"

"I have to do this," she said, eyeing me as if I was a great burden.

"Navani," he said, reaching for her.

She stepped back, pulled me up, and said, "If we want to ever truly defeat the supervillains, Andrew here is our only hope."

My mind swirled, confused by everything that had just come out of her mouth combined with the strange sight I'd just seen. Supervillains? Men and women vanishing, and where the hell was I? What had happened to my brother?

"Enough," I said, yanking myself from the woman's unnaturally strong grip. "Tell me what's happening right now!"

"You didn't tell him?" the strange man asked of the woman, who he'd called Navani.

"There was no time," Navani replied. "He was fighting Eclypse here, nearly killed himself to save the others."

The man turned a curious eye to me, then nodded. "Truly his father's son, no doubt."

"My father?" The mention of him here, like this, made no sense. "I'm going to tell you right now, my father went missing years ago, and I mean a lot of years. Even then, I'm adopted. So whatever weird game you're playing ends now. Who the hell are you, and how are you doing this?"

All I got for a response was a stare, as the two seemed to be debating how best to deal with me. It was only under their gaze, a barely noticeable glance down on her part, that I looked too and realized why I felt so free—I was completely nude!

"What the fuck—" I started, but then the man on the floor—Eclypse, apparently—suddenly jolted up, turned on me, and growled. His eyes glowed silver again, then a darkness started to take over until each eye was half silver, half black, and I had a sense of how he'd gotten his name. His fingers started to glow with a flame, but then the other man sighed, stepped up beside him, and placed a hand on the back of his neck.

Eclypse collapsed, a strange light flowing out of him and into this man.

"Xin," Navani said, "come with us."

"I wish that I could, but the only way we can find these others is with my help." With a deep breath, he walked over to the circle in the center of the room and knelt. "Go, now. I don't want you to see me like this."

She bit her lower lip, nodded, and then turned to stroll over to the ship. Xin bowed his head, light pulling from him and flowing toward the statues, and he said, "Call the first hero." The light intensified and I could see his skeleton within, hear echoing cries of torment, and then—

"ANDREW!" Navani shouted. "Move your ass!"

I'd responded so quickly to that phrase over the years and was in such a state of shock, that I immediately did as commanded. I high-tailed it out of there, following Navani up and into the craft. Only then did I pause to wonder when I'd get my clothes back and where I was going, as the doors were closing behind me. Of course, by then it was too late.

What the hell had I just gotten myself into?

2

The look in Navani's blue eyes when she turned to me was confusing—how do you interpret eyes that were completely blue? The ship was sailing through the sky, the image of a strange planet and even stranger metallic, pointed buildings were all disappearing below, but all I could focus on was this woman.

"What the fuck happened back there?" I asked.

She continued to stare, and then the blue of her eyes faded slightly so that they almost looked normal aside from a faint hue. Her hair now fell behind her, tied back in a ponytail but long, down to her ass, I assumed.

Instead of answering, she frowned, shook her

head as if trying to process something, and then stumbled past me.

"Hey," I said, following her. "I'm asking you a question."

With a glance back, she held up a hand and then motioned for me to stay close. "When we know we're safe."

"Safe?" I asked, but she was walking fast, not looking my way. We passed through a hallway and onto the bridge of the ship, where a transparent woman stood, hands behind her, staring out at the view ahead of us.

This confirmed my suspicion that I wasn't on Earth anymore, as large space stations were visible but blurry. On the display, the space stations were displayed more clearly, along with strange, far-off planets. In the distance was the white, flowing shape of the Milky Way galaxy, a mind-blowing sight when you've never left the place and you're seeing it for the very first time.

I took all this in with shock and awe, wondering why me, wondering what was going on back there on my home planet, so far away. Would my brother somehow have guessed what happened to me? Chad had always been a smart guy, but never one to go off on adventures like this. He'd probably assumed it was a medical-related hallucination and gone back for a bowl of rice soup and mint tea, knowing him.

Hell, it wasn't like I would've known how to react much better, had I seen him disappear through a portal and witnessed what had likely looked like a man exploding.

"Lamb," Navani said, earning a glance from the transparent woman. "What can we do for our friend here? Clothing, I mean."

Both women turned to look at me, standing there with my arms still spread in my motion of protestation, fully exposed. I blushed and covered myself, frowning. Lamb—as her name was, apparently—was damn hot, aside from the whole transparent thing. She had long, black hair and, in spite of being quite thin, wore something that looked like spandex, really showing off her hips and moving aside at the top to show ample cleavage. She had a red tint to her, though I wasn't sure if that was her or the lighting and her see-through state.

Lamb nodded and said, "Have a seat, Andrew."

"And that's another thing," I said. "How do you know my name?"

Both continued to stare at me, waiting, so I shook my head, unable to believe this. As I took a seat, I remembered to keep myself covered. The chair was actually comforting on my bare ass, with a gentle warmth to it.

"Choices are before you," Lamb said, finally turning away. "Will you need further assistance?" She turned to Navani, waiting.

"That'll do, thank you," Navani replied, bowing her head slightly.

With that, Lamb vanished. Navani stepped up next to the chair, eyes moving across my nude body, stopping at my hands where they covered myself.

"You mentioned clothing?" I said, not sure if I should feel offended at being treated like such a piece of meat.

She looked disappointed but nodded. "Lamb will be… helping you, in that regard."

I glanced around, confused. "She's a hologram?"

"That wasn't really her, no. That was part of her, a portion of her essence that has been merged with the ship to form an A.I., unlike anything you can imagine. And as for clothing, you certainly don't have to."

"It would make me feel more at ease," I said, unsure if she was joking.

She smiled, then nodded again. This time, the metal of the chair floated out like liquid metal, surrounding me, clinging to my body, soon covering my skin up to the neck. I tried to stand, but found I couldn't.

When I looked at her with fury, angry that she would try something like this, she laughed.

"Relax, Drew," she said. "You do prefer that over Andrew, no? Drew?"

"Lady, right now I couldn't give a fuck what you call me. I just want out of this. I want you to send me home, I want—"

"Clothes, yeah." She smiled and watched as the metal shimmered, and suddenly I could see a screen in front of me. I blinked, confused. In my Marine armor I'd had screens similar to this projected via my HUD, but not like this. I had to assume it was coming from a holo-screen in the chair or something. Basically, it showed various outfits with images of me in them.

"I don't understand," I admitted. "I'm online shopping here?"

"Pick one," she answered. "You'll see."

I glanced over, watching the way the light reflected off of the armor covering her tits, and then remembered myself. She noticed and raised an eyebrow. As my cock started to harden, she laughed and said, "Yes, Lamb, I noticed."

"Noticed what?" I asked. "And how are you talking to Lamb?"

"You can talk to me too," a voice said inside my head. "If you want, while you're on the ship. It'll be harder when you're not."

I gulped, confused as hell, but then noticed an outfit on-screen that I could feel right at home in. It was the Marine Corps green shirt and camo bottoms, along with boots and all. There was an option next to it, what looked like an upgrade, that resembled the armor I'd worn in my Space Marines days.

Once a Marine, always a Marine, I figured, so selected the first option. Comfort would be important as I got my bearings.

As soon as I'd selected it, the liquid metal around me formed into the outfit, even taking on a consistency like the clothes I'd been used to.

"Nice choice," Navani said, grinning. "Not as nice as the previous one, but nice."

"You mean when I was nude?"

She winked, then turned to the display with a heavy sigh. "We'll be exiting atmosphere soon. Exiting the protective barrier of the Citadel, though that is failing anyway. Then it will be up to you to save our world."

"Excuse me?"

She turned back to me, all mirth lost. Her eyes held a deep sorrow, a longing, and even a hint of confusion. The blue was coming back, and it was the most beautiful sight I'd ever seen, with her silvery-purple hair framing those eyes.

"Drew, what I'm about to tell you is going to be hard to swallow." She hesitated, grinned, and tried not to laugh. "Lamb, not the best time for a joke."

I frowned, but she waved it off.

"The point is, this is all about your father. Or both parents, maybe."

"As I said, I don't even know who my real father was."

"Right, but we do."

Now she had my attention. I tried to stand, and this time there was no resistance. A quick stretch, and then I turned to her, waiting.

"This is as good a time as any," she said, but looked like she was convincing herself. "Okay, you might want to sit down for this. It's not going to be easy to believe, but you're not going to have much choice in the matter, I'm sorry to say."

"I'd prefer to stand," I countered, not wanting to be bossed around.

"What you saw back there was the fall of the Citadel, or the start of its fall if we don't all succeed here. Xin and the others have sacrificed themselves to find new Elders, as they had already been defeated. With their last blast of energy they were able to summon Death Girl—I know, weird name but that's what she called herself once she took on the role—and she gathered the powers for them to be able to make this ultimate sacrifice. It's all… maybe best for another time, another story. But the simple version is that now they're finding new heroes to stand against Ranger and his forces.

"Only, none of that will ultimately matter if you don't fulfill your end of this equation."

"My destiny?" I scoffed. "Welcome to dreamland. Maybe I'll meet my princess and we'll live happily ever after?"

"It's a bit more complicated than that," she said. "Nobody said anything about destiny or…a single princess. Hell, we might fail here…we might not. It all comes down to DNA."

"Ah, the topic of my parents."

"Exactly. Your parents weren't just any regular supers, but the legendary tier one supers known as Apollo and Artemis." She paused for effect.

"Who?" I asked, assuming by the look on her face that those names should mean something to me.

"Oh, sorry, I just assumed you'd know they were gods, worshiped on Earth a long time ago."

"You've got the wrong brother if you want geek history discussions," I said.

"Not geek, Greek," she replied, forcing a smile that quickly faded at my glare.

Yeah, it annoyed me that she knew something about my planet I didn't. But Chad had always been the one fascinated with that stuff, while I was more of a realist and pragmatist. I studied military ethos, memorized stories about famous Medal of Honor recipients. Learned how to shoot the enemy and take the hill.

She pursed her lips, then said, "Suffice it to say, our two supers had taken on the names because they were tier one supers, practically worshipped, and their powers resembled those gods specifically. They even looked at love like old gods supposedly often did—to be shared. Our mother, me and my sisters, was the same way. She would travel the planets of our galaxy, finding mates and... er, we'll come to that. The point is, they were powerful beyond belief until they vanished."

"Vanished?" I asked, ignoring the talk of shared love, as curious as the topic made me.

She nodded. "The questions surrounding that event are many. The answers, few. All I can say is that they had two boys, we now know."

"Okay...?"

"You, Drew. You and Chad." She frowned, giving me a look I'd come to hate over the years. While I wasn't as smart as my brother, I didn't deserve condescending looks like that, and the words coming out of her mouth were nonsense. No way was I a son of some god-like superhuman.

"Maybe it's time I should leave," I said, glancing at the door.

"You can't," she said.

"So I'm a prisoner here?"

She shook her head, sighed, and said, "The simple truth is this—you have the DNA in you of the most powerful supers ever known. That's incredibly rare."

"What you're saying is," I asked, leaning forward excitedly, "I'm going to be put into some sort of superhero academy, trained to use my powers, and ultimately go up against the evilest supervillain to ever live?" As nerdy as it sounded, the idea thrilled me. It totally reminded me of some super old nerd-fest movie about a boy and a magic school that my brother had been obsessed with.

"Not at all," Navani said. "But…good imagination. The thing is, you might have superpowers. You survived the flames from Eclypse, and hit him with something interesting, but you're not strong enough. Definitely not enough to ultimately destroy the evil of this galaxy and save the universe."

"So then we're wasting our time here," I pointed

out, pissed. Just another reminder to not get my hopes up.

"Not at all." She stepped close enough that I could smell a faint scent like lilies and waterfalls if that made sense. It didn't, but that's the image, or sensation, that her smell filled me with.

"I'm not following," I admitted.

She bit her lip for this part, the otherwise perfect posture bending slightly, and then she reached out, suddenly and unexpectedly, and took my hand in hers. Her metal armor moved back from her hand as it reached for mine so that I could feel the warmth of her skin.

"It's asking a lot of you, I know," she said.

I stared down at her hand holding mine, then up to her eyes. "You haven't asked anything of me, yet."

"Yet...but now." Her other hand came to mine too so that she held my one hand with both of hers, and her eyes were wide. "There was my mother, as I mentioned, a super so strong they considered her a goddess, too, and she had several daughters. No sons. The thought is, with all of the power the enemy is bringing against us, we need a super that would be a combination of the so-called god that was your father, and the goddess that was my mother, and that of my sisters. Well, mostly half-sisters."

"Holy fuck," I blurted out, suddenly starting to understand where this was going, and why she was holding my hand. "You're going to kill me and take my DNA, using it to make a mutant version of you and me somehow."

She dropped my hand, holding hers up to her face as it scrunched in confusion. "What?!"

"That's where you were going, right?" I protested, stepping back. "Well, it's not going to happen!"

"No, you big, sexy idiot." She laughed, then looked at me as if debating whether I was joking, then laughed again. "We supers have a very, very low chance of getting pregnant. Comes with the territory of being very hard to kill, I guess. Maybe something to do with the effects of our sun, which gave us these powers in the first place. Except for my mother, where it seemed the sun had the opposite effect, allowing for increased fertility. Maybe that worked for others in our galaxy, but it's quite rare if so. Since I have many half-sisters that I've traced across the galaxy, while you only have the one brother, I have to assume. But yes, all of this... it's speculation to a degree. What I do know is that someone with your genes needs to have a baby with someone with our genes."

"A baby..."

"That's right. The enemy has already sent one of

their greatest warriors to hunt us down. We'll have to find the others, my sisters, and half-sisters, and save them. Along the way, we...hope that you, well... we hope that you'll do your damned best to work on impregnating us."

My chest rose and fell quickly. My cock shifted as blood flooded into my groin at the thought of what she'd just proposed. I opened my mouth to speak. No words came out.

Had this sexy-ass lady just asked me if I'd be willing to fly around her galaxy saving damsels in distress and then having sex with them? It was confusing, it was ridiculous...and it was sexy as fuck. Every man's fantasy, in a very twisted and outlandish way.

We started exiting atmosphere and I stumbled back into the chair as the ship shook around me. Navani fell back into the chair in front of mine, but then spun it around so she could face me.

"Do you understand, Drew?" she asked, speaking loudly so I could hear her over it all.

I took a deep breath, and nodded. "Except, if it's hard to impregnate supers... are there no people on the planets? Not many? How many sisters are there?"

"The number of sisters I'm unsure of, and I don't even know most of them. We've tracked down only a few." She took a deep breath. "I've told you about rumors that certain supers, including my mother, were more easily able to procreate than others, but there's even a rumor that my mother's powers allowed others to be more susceptible. They gave her the name Arianrhod."

"Doesn't sound so Greek," I said, finally wanting to show off I knew something too. "In fact, wouldn't Aphrodite be more appropriate there?"

"Different planets have tended to fascinate themselves with different parts of Earth lore and history," she pointed out, frowning at being put off track. "Some don't care one lick, others are completely fascinated by it all. Point is, it goes that she could kind of bless others by being nearby or something, so they too could have children. She met your mother at one point, they say... and the rest is history."

"All because of the sun?"

"The powers, yes. The citadel harnesses those. My theory is still that the sun just worked differently on my mother, but... some have speculated that genetic tinkering was involved. Either way, childbirth is rare. A great responsibility, for those able to participate."

I blinked, now understanding why the mother had felt obliged to have so many children, and why the supers had considered her to be so important to their continued expansion. If my genes were truly descended from these gods, I also had this responsibility. In a sense.

"One last thing… if there are these super-powerful tier one superheroes out there, why aren't they trying to save the universe instead of us? I mean, especially… me."

"Gone," she said bluntly. "Nobody knows where, but they vanished around the same time of Ranger's arrival."

"Fuck."

"Yes, Drew. Fuck." She stared at me for a long, hard minute, then said, "Do you accept?"

With a hungry glance at her lips, imagining my own caressing them, then with flashes through my mind of her warm body pressed against mine, how could I say no? The thought of her nipples in my mouth and the throbbing in my cock as I fantasized about the moment confirmed it. The way she was looking at me showed that her mind was in the same place.

"Hell yes, I accept," I said, then was pressed back in my seat, unable to hide the bulge in my pants as we emerged into space.

3

We flew into space, Lamb appearing and smiling at us as the jolting stopped.

"Enjoy the rest of the ride," she said with a grin, looking first at me and then Navani. "Gravity shifters are in place, all sensations should be as if we were back on planet. If you experience problems, of any sort," she glanced back my way this time, a hint of humor in her eyes, "I'll be happy to help."

"Thank you, Lamb," Navani said as the woman faded.

"She's very lifelike, for an A.I.," I said, trying to figure out how we'd bring up the subject of sleeping together, but very confused about the whole situation.

"Maybe I didn't explain her situation well enough earlier?" Navani said. "Her powers, when she sacrificed herself with the others—"

"Wait, so she's dead?"

"None of them are, yet," Navani said, frowning at my interruption. "They've used the Citadel as a way to channel their powers into finding new heroes. I thought we went over this?"

"How's that relate to the A.I.?"

Navani sighed. "She's not an A.I., exactly. Merged, remember? She can really see you, still has her thoughts and whatnot, even kind of feel you in a way." Her eyes roamed over my body but in a curious way this time. Maybe even a jealous way?

"Explain," I demanded.

"The way the suit works, it's nanotech, or biotech or whatever, but fueled by her powers. In a way, that is her essence left behind, and it can work as defensive clothing. She'll serve as a shield, protecting you against shots to a degree. At least, as long as the shield can last. And while you're close to the ship, I believe, she can help in other ways."

"Shall I show you?" a voice whispered in my ear.

I jumped, looking around, and then saw the way Navani was holding back a laugh. "That's her, isn't it?"

"Tell him he can speak directly to me," Lamb said, her voice coming from all around now.

"You heard her," Navani said. "She can choose to speak just to you or me, individually, or everyone aboard this ship."

"Are there others?"

She shook her head. "No need, not with her on board. But there will be."

"Ah, right. The other women I'm supposed to…impregnate."

Her cheeks actually flushed at that, but she didn't look away. "That's correct." After a moment, she added, "Listen, I know it's awkward. It's just as weird for me, and I can assure you it will be for the others."

"They don't know yet."

"Oh, about that. No." She turned, looking off into space. "We could just try, you and me. But I know the chances, and I know this is bigger than us. If the universe's fate depends on your seed and our wombs, who are we to argue?"

"Holy shit, did you just say those words?" I couldn't help but laugh. "My seed? What the fuck?"

"How else should I say it?" she asked, glaring at me as she stood from her seat and took off for the door. She paused at my side, staring down at me. "You think it's easy to talk to some stranger about him shooting cum up inside me? Is that the crass way you'd prefer? Well it's my fucking body, and those of my sisters, so I'll say seed if I want and you can shut the hell up."

With that, she stormed out of there.

"I'm…" I was about to say 'sorry,' but the door slid shut behind her. For a moment I sat there, staring at the door, and then burst into laughter. "My seed. My seed?!"

"You're being an insensitive twat," Lamb said, suddenly appearing in front of me at the same time as a pressure started on my balls. "You hurt her, I hurt you. Let's start this off by being clear about that."

My laughter was cut off, my smile gone as I scooted back. But now, there was nothing on my crotch, just the pressure as if someone had a foot pressed against my nuts, ready to perform the nutcracker.

Lamb's translucent face leaned into mine, her black hair falling around her face and almost framing mine, she was so close. "Do I make myself clear?"

I nodded.

"Good," she continued. "It's not easy for her, you know. Would it be for you, if you were in her shoes? She doesn't know you. On your planet, you could be a complete scumbag."

"Or married with children," I pointed out.

She frowned. "But the records said—"

"Relax, I don't. I'm just saying, this is crazy for both of us."

"We all know," she admitted, the harshness fading from her voice, her frown relaxing. "But...am I wrong to assume that you Earther men like sex?"

"Of course we do," I admitted. "I'm definitely not complaining here, just...confused? Maybe a bit nervous."

"I see." She leaned back now, crossing her arms in a way that pushed up her cleavage even more. I'd done my share of VR sex games in my day, I admit, but this was on a whole new level. Her tongue brushed gently across her upper lip, then she cocked her head, looking at me. "I hadn't considered that you might need coaxing, or help. But it makes sense, and we can accommodate that."

One of her eyebrows went up and she smiled, and at the same moment, the pressure on my balls changed to an entirely different sensation altogether. Instead of the threat of pain, it felt like hands were caressing me, massaging my thighs, working in and gently brushing against the edge of my package. More hands began to knead my back, and at once my back was arched, my legs spread as I invited those hands to grab my cock. My mind was completely at ease, though somewhere back there I was vaguely aware that there were no actual hands.

"How…?" I tried to ask but instead shuddered as the invisible hands moved across my shaft, like a woman accidentally brushing across it, or when one pretends to but is really testing to see if you're hard. Believe me, by that point I was.

"It's technically not me," she said. "I belonged to another, in life. In this state, we've left parts of us behind to help with the transition, and this…" With a smile, she watched me as I moaned, my muscles clenched, the hands taking me in full, "…this is simply the suit responding to your desires, with a little prodding from me. I suppose it's what it *would* have felt like if it were really me, though."

"That's… that's…" I wasn't listening, I just wanted it to keep going. But suddenly, it stopped. I realized my eyes were closed, so I opened them to see that she was gone. A glance over my shoulder revealed that the doors were open again, Navani standing there staring at me.

"What's this?" she asked.

"I was showing him how the suit could help… prepare him," Lamb said, not appearing.

"And you think I need that?"

"Not you, him. He's not entirely comfortable either. Or… wasn't."

Navani frowned, turning my way as if to challenge the statement. Instead, she strode over to me, stared me down, then leaned in and planted her lips on mine. It was awkward, forced, unnatural. My eyes met hers, and I saw it too.

When she stood, she said, "Dammit," and then stormed off again. This time she paused at the door and said, "Lamb, stay out of it. I'll calm him the fuck down."

Holy hell, was my mind swirling. My cock was still rock hard, the memory of those hands fresh in my mind, and now I was stuck with that horrible feeling that this wasn't going to go well at all with Navani. That kiss had been like kissing a sister. It didn't work. At all.

I'd been in only one situation like that before, when I met this amazingly beautiful woman at a get-together with some friends, and one of my buddies had convinced me to hit on her. There was something off about the whole situation. You know when a woman is insanely hot, but you're not sure if you're really attracted to her? Like she's clearly a ten, but you can't imagine the two of you rolling around in the sheets, no matter how hard you tried? It was like that. But she was open-minded, and we went out for a drink. She thought I was fun, loved the idea that I was a Marine, and I think that was enough for her to come over to my place. We had just settled down to watch a movie when she turned and pulled out my cock.

"What are you doing?" I'd asked, totally caught off guard.

"I've always wanted to go down on a Marine," she explained, and I watched with amazement as this perfect ten took my limp dick in her mouth. Her large, brown eyes—I think she was part Egyptian, part something else like Indian, maybe—stared up at me as she did, and all I could think was that this girl never would've even talked to me back in high school, and now she had my limp dick in her mouth.

And that's all that happened, because no matter how hard she licked, sucked, or tugged, it wouldn't go up. A mental block, for sure. I know it worked fine, because the next night I met a seven at a club, maybe she was even a six, I don't know, and she'd gone down on me behind the stairs out back. No problems then.

This, I imagined, was something like that whole former experience. It was my fault. I was hung up on her beauty, maybe feeling a bit inadequate.

All that time, sitting there, I hadn't noticed when Lamb had returned. There she was though, watching me with a skeptical face. When she saw that I had finally noticed, she scoffed.

"Wow, we're all royally fucked, aren't we?"

"What?" I asked.

"You're just sitting there when you should be going after her. Jackass."

Of course, she was right. I stumbled up, tucked my boner in the belt of my pants, hoping it would go away soon, and went back out through the doors to find Navani. I wasn't yet sure what I'd say once I found her, but knew I needed to find a workaround here.

Fuck that. I had a beautiful woman ready to show me what it means to be a man, to toss me back and let me cum inside her as many times as I could, and I was being a dick about it. Excuse me, that wasn't about to keep happening, I told myself. I was a fucking Marine! It was time to go into her room or wherever she was, apologize, and whip out my dick. Or maybe I'd talk to her first, make it sensual. I didn't exactly have it figured out, but the point was that I was going to make it right. If I played my cards right, I'd have my flag planted very soon in a garden of silvery-purple pubic hair.

That was a thought! One that instantly hit me, visually and physically, as a chill ran up my spine. Maybe getting over my hold-ups wouldn't be as difficult as I'd thought.

I wasn't even three paces from the doors before

the ship took its first hit, sending me slamming into the far wall.

"Battle stations," Lamb called, voice carrying throughout the ship. "The hunters have found their prey—us. Let's see if we can escape them, shall we?"

Navani appeared a moment later, eyes blazing blue, and walked right past me without a second glance. I looked up and down the hall, wondering where she kept storming off to, but when a second hit sent me sprawling across the floor, I followed to return to my chair.

The display was lit up, attacking vessels all over us. We were definitely fucked. If anything had been about to happen, this was the biggest cock-block of all times.

4

The ships were zooming past, much faster than ours. Navani and Lamb were in control, sending out shots and maneuvering, the shields flaring each time we took a hit.

"We're going to die," I mumbled. As much as I didn't want to believe it, I'd been in enough firefights to know that, when outnumbered like that, it was only a matter of time.

"Don't be so sure," Navani said.

The ship moved faster than I would have thought possible. No ship back on Earth could've handled this, not even one from the notorious fleet of three hundred. We flew on through space, but it was clear that, somehow, the other ships were even faster.

"Can someone tell me who the hell they are?" I shouted, starting to panic as the shields fizzled time and again as shots connected.

"Followers of Ranger, the enemy of the Citadel," Lamb said, appearing at my side. As the attacks kept coming and we swept around to fire back, she continued. "He's set up a regime of supervillains, able to travel on a dimension inaccessible to us, but able to attack our defenses. While they defeated the Citadel, they must wait for him and his army to arrive. One move he recently made was to divert his powers toward a prison ship full of the most notorious supervillains alive. He promised them freedom and power if they would help him fight, but we've sent a team to deal with it." For a moment she looked distant, confused. "That is all I can say on the matter, for now. But other missions of his are in play to secure his points of power, such as making a move to destroy you and your brother."

"Because of this whole DNA connection to the super known as Apollo. Yeah, I get it."

She continued, explaining that he had set up various supervillains with different armies around the galaxy, making moves on other planets, though the majority of them focused on the Citadel. As she spoke, though, I started tuning out—the ships were gathering too fast, gaining, and more and more seemed to be showing up. I honestly couldn't see a way out of this.

And while the ships were too many, starting to surround us, even targeting us and locked in, Navani was smiling.

"What?" I asked.

She glanced my way, but before she could respond Lamb said, "Incoming call."

"Accept," Navani replied.

The screen flashed to show a new image in the middle. A large man looked from Navani to me, his eyes a creepy, glowing green. All of his skin had the look of someone who'd been lightly burned, and he had no hair. It could have been pathetic, if not for the size of him and those wild eyes.

"Goros," Navani said, spittle practically flying at the display. "So, he sent you as his lackey?"

"Hand him over," Goros said. "His brother will be dealt with soon enough, and this will all be over. No use prolonging it."

"You can't have him," she grumbled.

"Him, then you. Of course, I might as well deal with the rest of the sisters while I'm at it. Mine is a grand vision, Navani, one you couldn't possibly hope to understand. Ranger isn't destroying your way of life, he's fixing it. With everyone in their place according to power positions, we will be free to go about our business without confusion over who is what. Ranger is our savior, but you must be destroyed, all of you, so that we may all thrive in the future."

"You're sick," she told him, shaking her head. "Shove this up your ass."

She nodded to Lamb and a second later a barrage flew at the enemy ships.

"Preparing for jump space," Lamb said.

The ship lurched, moving fast, going along in a circle among the enemy so that they fired upon themselves as they tried to hit us.

"Who is he?" I asked as Navani took the pilot seat and called out for Lamb to be ready.

"One of these supervillains who've appeared out of nowhere, lately. It's odd," she said as she dodged a strike, working to pull the ship up and fire back, "all these powerful supers, appearing like this. Usually, we have records, keep tabs at the Citadel. But these guys who're under Ranger, they don't show up anywhere. Ready, Lamb?"

"Affirmative," Lamb said.

"And Ranger is the ultimate enemy?" I asked. "The one we need to kill?"

"Right now, we just need to escape, then focus on your mission. There are worse evils out there that the offspring must deal with. Evils only now growing, lurking—"

"You sound like you're out of one of my little brother's nerd fest movies."

She glared, then said, "Lamb, how's our connection to Hadrian?"

"Coming up on the jump spot in three, two, one…"

Navani stood, hands out, and her eyes flared. She moved her hands and holo-screens came up from the display. As she put in coordinates, the ship started to shake, blue flowing out from her eyes until the whole ship was blue light, and then a figure appeared as if floating in front of it, wearing red and gold space armor. He turned, no helmet, and I saw that half of his face was disfigured, but his smile was pleasant, his power overwhelming.

"I have your coordinates," the figure said, and then we were pressing through, only light visible so that I had to close my eyes to stop from going blind. With another jolt, it was over, and we were through.

"What…happened?" I asked.

"You've just seen our gateway super," she explained. "One of the supers who is making all of this possible, thanks to his sacrifice."

"And Navani's got locator sight," Lamb explained.

"She's able to spot targets through walls, but also able to pinpoint locations of people.

"It's why I was chosen for this mission," Navani added. "Although, I didn't know I'd be going up against Goros."

"But this…Hadrian? He seemed fine to me."

"Like Lamb, he is no more, not in his entirety," she explained. "What you saw was his essence, his soul, almost, lingering behind to guide us."

"So his ghost." I turned to see the form of Lamb. "And you…you're like a strange A.I. ghost."

"No," Lamb said, then turned to Navani. "He's not getting it."

"Does he need to?" she countered.

Lamb faded, with a shake of her head.

Navani and I looked out at the breadth of clear space around us—no enemy ships within sight.

"We did it," she said, as if only now realizing it. "We escaped."

Navani turned with a wide smile, excitement dancing like water across the blue of her eyes. Only, she paused, looking unsure whether she should give me a high five or go for another kiss.

I grinned. "Nice work, hotshot. We're in the clear?"

"As far as I know, they don't have a super who

can create gates like that, so yes, we're safe. For now. We're also much closer to our target."

"Then, maybe we could, I don't know…take a walk?" I gestured to the door.

"You know," she said, giving me a wink, "Lamb can hear us everywhere."

"It's not about that," I protested. "It's more like… the act of taking a walk. Like a date."

Her right eyebrow arched, but then she smiled. "Okay, yeah."

She led the way, and I followed. When we reached the hallway, she turned to me and held out her hand. I chuckled, but wrapped my arm in it.

"We might as well be as friendly as we can," she said. "I mean, we shouldn't hold back, right?"

"I agree. This doesn't have to be awkward."

We walked for a bit, silence returning and making it totally awkward. We turned and she led me up to a higher level of the ship, walking up the stairs in a way that made it impossible not to stare at her ass. Yes, it was covered in her armor, but it was tight, and my imagination worked its magic.

At the top, she said, "You go first next time."

I grinned. Our little attempt at flirtation? There was certainly something I could say back here, but dammit, her beauty made me feel like an idiot. She cocked her head and I realized I was staring, so turned to look around and froze in awe.

We were surrounded by a viewing deck, the stars around us unlike anything back home. The planet we'd just left was a fluorescent green when viewed from out here. Other galaxies were within sight, ones I had never been able to see from Earth, some flowing like fire, others mixtures of orange and purple.

Staring out at it all, I had to wonder if my brother was okay, what was going on back home with him and the whole bank situation.

"My brother, he was able to see you?" I asked.

"I don't have a cloaking power or anything like that," she said. "Wait…your brother?"

"He was there, at the bank." I turned to her, surprised. "You didn't know?"

"We've been tracking you," she admitted. "With your military records and all that. At least, my team was—I believe Xin has a mission for him, but it wasn't my responsibility to take him with us."

"So he's been taken through this portal thing too?"

"Or will be soon, yes. I'm not sure." She stared into my eyes. "You're worried about him?"

"Of course I am. He's my little bro. And, that whole incident at the bank."

She grinned. "Relax, we were fast. The nature of portals like that, they're more like stargates, they kind of slow down time as you're traveling through them. Of course, he might've seen, depending on his superpowers."

I laughed. "He doesn't have superpowers."

"You don't know," she countered. "He's also the son of Apollo. I believe Xin has sensed something great in him."

Those words hit me hard. My little brother, a superhero? He'd always been so...mundane. But at least he was safe.

"Wait a minute," I said. "The man attacking... Eclypse, what was he doing there?"

"My guess? Trying to draw you out."

"But he didn't attack me. It was like—"

"I know," she interrupted. "But maybe he knew your brother was there, too. Maybe he wanted you to be in danger so your brother would reveal himself. Honestly? I don't know for sure, but I'm glad we stopped him."

She took my arm again, standing at my side. Then, slowly, she leaned her head against my shoulder.

"Tell me about yourself," she said.

"Like what?"

"Surprise me."

"Well," I wracked my brain, trying to think about what might impress her. "I was in the Marines back home."

"Yes, I know that part. But… why? Why did you join? Why did you leave?"

I frowned. "I joined to see space, I guess?" With a laugh, I put my hand on her forearm, the one clutching my arm. "Guess that part is happening now, much more than I'd ever anticipated. And maybe… to meet girls."

"Both accomplished," she said, giving me a grin as she lifted her head to look into my eyes. "You're going to see more of space than you could've imagined. You're going to have more fun with—not girls—but women, than you can probably handle."

"I can handle myself," I said, giving her a glance.

"We'll see," she replied, but looked away. I had kind of thought that would be my cue, my chance to make a move. Apparently, she wasn't having it. I tried thinking back to past relationships, how I'd made moves and what had worked, but nothing was coming to mind. It had always happened naturally, meeting at a bar, dancing, strolling out into the night and catching the smile of a beautiful lady.

Being pulled through a portal and told you're responsible for trying to impregnate a bunch of ladies who have less than a one-percent chance of getting pregnant? Not exactly a proper mood setter. And honestly, right now she wasn't helping. Maybe Lamb was right, that this was harder on Navani than I realized.

For a long time, we stood there, her arm in mine, staring out at the stars. Then I turned to her and said, "Beautiful."

"Aren't they," she said, dreamily.

"You," I corrected her. "You're beautiful. Stunning. As weird as all this could be, I'm looking at you and thinking I'm the luckiest guy alive, and that if this journey is with you—"

She held a finger to my lips, a pained expression crossing over her, and then she turned away.

"What is it?" I asked.

"Don't. Not like this." She took her arm from mine, then walked off a couple of steps. "You can't say things like that to me and make this work."

"I'm really not following."

"Do you honestly think I'll be able to stand by while you fuck other women if you've convinced me to fall for you first? Do you really believe all of this, a date, your compliments, your beautiful fucking face, won't make me fall for you if we go down this road?"

"You're the one who brought me here. I'm just trying to figure it out as I go."

"Well, try this on for size. Be nice, be comforting,

but... I think we should wait to, you know, do the deed until we have at least one of my sisters involved. That way it'll be easier on all of us."

Damn, I wanted her at that moment more than I'd ever wanted anyone in my whole life. She was not only turning me down but saying we had to wait until we had another woman to join the bed?

"If—" I started, trying to think of a way to make it happen now, but she held up a hand, walking off. "Sorry, it has to be this way."

I sighed, turned back to the view, and said, "Lamb? I don't suppose this suit could help me out here."

"You mean you want me to jack you off?" Lamb said, appearing in the glass in front of me. She shook her head, slowly. "Sorry, Big D, we need to save your *seed*," she smirked, "for when it matters."

"Fucking hell," I said, feeling like my dick was going to explode, it was pumped so full of blood. "And... big what?"

"You know, you're strong, your name is Drew."

"Andrew actually," I corrected her. "But Drew works, sure. Not so certain about 'Big D.'"

She shrugged, vanishing and leaving me to stare out at the stars by myself, a raging hard-on reminding me that I had a very strange mission to accomplish here, and they weren't letting me do it.

When she was halfway down the stairs, she paused, turned back to me, and put on a sneaky grin that didn't fit her at all.

"What?" I asked.

"There," she said, pointing to a bright star. "We're almost to our destination."

"Oh, wonderful," I replied, although I was kind of excited to see who this sister would be. Part of me felt let down, however. I'd expected her to say 'fuck it, let's give it a go.' Not yet, apparently.

Knowing it would be soon, if we could get this sister on the same page or if I could seduce her, I followed her down to get suited up and ready to go.

5

At the ship's door, I looked around, then glanced down at my outfit of Marine-style battle armor and said, "Lamb, should I be wearing this?"

"He really is new, isn't he?" Lamb said, and a moment later I was wearing pants and a shirt with a jacket. It wasn't so different from the clothes I wore back home in my off time, and the jacket felt like nice leather. I shook my head, amazed at how they did that.

"Stay close," Navani said to me. "I don't think we'll find trouble here, but in case we do, I need to know you're nearby so I can save your ass."

"Or maybe I'll save yours."

"You can do whatever you want to my ass," she said, "but…Oh, never mind. That was bad."

"I like the meaning, but the delivery, yeah." I grinned, but she'd already moved on, given up. At least she was trying, I thought, trying to figure out how I could up my game here, too. We needed to be comfortable when the moment came. Not rigid, like we were at that moment.

She opened the ramp, and we descended into the landing dock of a city with buildings that resembled rolling hills, only they seemed to be made out of glass and minerals. Some sparkled in the afternoon light, others just shone brightly.

Navani waved a hand over her face, and her eyes appeared like anyone else's. "Okay, ready."

"Hold up," I said. "What?"

She cocked her head, then said, "Oh, the eyes? It's a disguise."

"I get that, but why not all the time?"

"When they're blue, I have my true sight. My powers. Why would I opt to have that off?"

"Sure."

"You don't like how my blue eyes look?"

I opened my mouth to respond, but thinking about it, there was something weirdly sexy about them. All of this, and the cute dress she was wearing —while not half as revealing as the purple and gray skin-tight armor she wore aboard the ship—made me think of her more like any other woman back home, aside from the purple in her hair.

And as I was about to answer, to pay her a compliment, she turned and walked off.

"Not keeping up," she said over her shoulder, so I jogged over.

"Okay, my intel showed two of them here. The first one is this way." She turned at one of the glass dunes, leading me along a path lined with short, orange shrubs.

"How's that work?" I asked.

"My sight? I have to have something of the person's or have been in recent physical contact with them. In this case, we had some of their belongings in an evidence box from when they were last arrested."

"You said they were superheroes."

"Heroes get arrested too," she said, "if they step out of line. But also, no, I don't know if I said that. The sisters are all descended from a very powerful superhero, but that doesn't mean we're all heroes."

Several men and women exited one of the buildings through a door that rose, and I was able to catch a glimpse inside. There seemed to be a whole city down there. But the door we stopped at was different. The entire dome was glass with a bright red light shining through it, several women standing about in various states of revealing clothing.

"Don't tell me," I whispered. "You're stopping by here to buy me a lap dance?"

She frowned. "This is where she should be." With a quick return of her blue vision, she glanced around, one hand in her pocket holding something, and then nodded. "In there."

We entered, and Navani pointed out the person we'd come for. She wasn't at all what I was expecting. When you talk about superheroes, you think good, maybe even godly. The woman I was looking at had on the shortest mini-skirt you could think of, a blouse that was unbuttoned enough to show she had cute little perky breasts and no bra, and nipples that were visibly hard. Her forehead had lined tattoos, and what looked like tiny horns were barely hidden under her straight, black hair. As she drew closer, I saw they weren't tattoos at all, as they glowed slightly.

She glanced my way as she passed, then at Navani, and frowned. When she sat down at a bar next to a man, she whispered something in his ear, then reached down, unzipped his pants, and started jacking him off! She was clearly doing it in a way that was meant not to be seen by the bartender, but didn't care if others saw. There she was, this woman we were going to try to seduce, and she had some dude's cock in her hand, stroking it.

I blinked, trying to erase the image from my mind, and turned away. "What the fuck?"

"At least we know she'll be on the easier side," Navani said with a chuckle, still watching.

When I turned again to look, the woman was glaring at us.

"Maybe we should go," I whispered in Navani's ear.

"You know the mission, how important it is."

"Listen," I leaned in, the strict Marine in me coming out, "she has another man's cock in her hand. Right now. I can fucking see it. You think I'm going to fuck her after this?"

She turned to me, blue eyes going bright, and grabbed me by the wrist, pulling me toward the back and then close. "Listen—"

"Hey, you two," a large man said, stepping around the bar. "Not in the hall, how many times do I have to tell people? In there."

He gestured to a curtained-off room, and only then did I notice the sounds of flesh slapping flesh, the muted moans. No way was I going into one of those sex booths, I thought, but Navani was already pulling me back. She pushed aside the curtain and then pulled me through so that we were both in a blacklight-lit room. I guess they had the lights so you'd know there weren't any fluids around, that they were super clean or whatever, but the whole concept made me feel even more sleazy.

"This is how you're going to do it?" I asked, gesturing to the mattress on the raised platform. "A sex capsule?"

She slapped me. The woman slapped me!

"Listen, Drew. I'm going to say this right now, one time, and then it's going to be out of my system. You aren't going to complain about shit, because me and you, we'll have an understanding. Clear?"

I rubbed my cheek. "Crystal."

"Good. I don't give two shits if she's rubbing his cock on your face while you fuck her. She's one of the sisters, which means she's as likely as the rest of us to be the one you impregnate. She could be the mother of the only super capable of standing up to the enemy, do you comprehend this?"

"Yes, but…for the record, I'm not letting anyone rub someone else's cock anywhere near me. Not happening."

"It was an example," she said with a roll of her eyes. "Point is, don't be a bitch."

I remembered what Lamb had said about this not being easy on any of us, and nodded. "Agreed. I'll suck it up."

With a disgusted expression, she motioned around the room and said, "Bad word choice, considering where we are."

I laughed. "Okay, fine. How do you want to do this? You go talk to her, or I slip her some money, and we go from there?"

"Fuck," Navani said as she pulled the curtain slightly aside. "It's not like I expected this. But... her records said she has issues. Maybe we do just offer her money to come with us if she's doing all this for credit anyway."

"Shouldn't she want to be part of it though, if she's a superhero and all?"

"Not all supers are heroes, and just because she's got the DNA, doesn't mean she's inherited our mom's way of thinking." She pulled back from the curtain and pointed.

"What?"

She stepped away from the curtain, bit her lip, and knelt. With a quick movement, she was leaning, in, bobbing her head up and down as she mumbled, "She's coming, just go along with it."

Those blue eyes looked up at me. I imagined my dick in her mouth, wishing it was actually happening, but for the moment simply nodded, grabbed her by the hair, and moaned. The curtain opened, and I pretended not to notice as my fingers clenched in her hair, maybe getting too much into it. When she grabbed my ass and squeezed, it fucking hurt. And...yes, it felt damn good.

A rush of adrenaline and hormones shot through me. If we'd been really into this, I would have lifted her up right then and there, pinned her to the wall, and showed her how a Marine sets his flag. Every muscle in my body wanted it, clenching and unclenching, warm, tingling sensations taking over. When I saw it in my mind's eye, the image I created of her titties bouncing as she rode my dick, it was almost real. Every ounce of me wanted her, and as my breathing intensified, so did a strength I'd never known I had, like I could climb Mount Everest in a sprint and then jump off the fucking top, wings spread wide for the sky to take me.

Only, I didn't have wings, and Navani, unfortunately, wasn't really fucking me or even giving me head.

Someone cleared her throat.

The first sight when I opened my eyes was Navani, staring up at me with shock. Maybe I'd gotten a little too into the charade? The next thing I saw was the woman standing there, holding the curtain back with one hand, her other on her waist. She had an eyebrow raised, eyes full of annoyance.

"Bullshit," she said. "Good acting on his part, but you think I don't know the sound of a blowjob?"

We hesitated, Navani glancing up at me, and then she turned to reveal that my dick was indeed still in my pants. "Okay, you caught us."

"Yay for me," the woman said. "Now mind explaining why you're eyeballing me one minute, pretending to give head to this guy while hiding the next?"

Navani hesitated, glanced at me—so hot, that view—and then stood. "See, the thing is, we've wanted to spice things up a bit between us, and we thought you might be able to help us."

"What?" I said before stopping myself and nodding instead.

"That so?" the woman asked, looking me over. "What'd you have in mind? A blowjob while you watch? A good fuck?"

"Actually," Navani said and shrugged, "yes, all of the above."

"Right. Okay, whip it out then."

My eyes went wide and I hesitated, but Navani stepped back in. "We were actually hoping you'd come back with us and do it in our room. More comfortable, right? Room for me, too, if that's allowed."

The woman eyed her, chuckled, and said, "Yeah? I

might have to charge more than usual, but…" She gave me another look and grinned. "I'm Sakurai, by the way. Figured we should get that out of the way before we fuck."

"Ah… Drew," I said.

"Now, where is this room?"

"Not far, it's—"

Screams interrupted her, and not the good kind. As she turned to see what was going on, a sound like sizzling bacon with the smell to match came, growing louder and more intense, and then a large explosion shook the place.

We stepped out into the hall as naked men and women darted out of booths, running for their lives but not sure which way to go so they were bumping into each other, some falling and getting trampled underfoot. A burst of green light hit one, like a bolt of electricity only focused, unending, until the person basically melted. More attackers were rushing in, and a small army was beginning to form, armed with guns. They started to mow down those they could before they were taken out by orange blasts from the bartender's hands.

"Holy shit," I muttered, while Sakurai and Navani went into kickass mode. Navani pulled a blaster from her newly-reformed armor, rolling aside as her eyes scanned the room, and she started firing.

Although her shots were aimed right at the wall, they went through. Muffled shouts of pain followed as at least one corpse falling against the wall, I guessed by the thud.

I had ducked back into the room, or sex closet, and was watching when I recognized someone. It was the man from the display screen earlier, the one who was with the fleet that had attacked us before our jump—Goros. Navani had said we were safe, that they didn't have the capacity to jump. So, then, how come he was here?

Goros had his hands out, his black and green cloak flailing out behind, and another burst of green lightning shot out, taking down three in its path. He turned on Sakurai, and I was ready to step in, but she wasn't so defenseless. With a thrust of her hand, I heard the sound of metal rattling, as a sword shot through the air and seemed to form as it flew. Then it was full, and the hilt landed in her hand. It was similar to a katana, only with a thicker blade and more pronounced at the top. Its hilt bore a resemblance to a dragon, and as she thrust, it became clear why. Her tattoos lit up, and the sword seemed to come to life, light and shadows mixing around it until there appeared to be a large dragon circling it and moving out to attack her enemies.

Shooters fell as she charged them, sword

slashing and the dragon of light spinning, encircling, exploding. Holy fuck, this was bordering on the hottest and scariest sight I'd ever witnessed. Her skirt flipped around her as she fought, tight ass exposed, and suddenly I wanted to be the one to ensure she came with us. Was it sexual? Not in the back of my mind, but right then my hormones were definitely driving me. Otherwise, I wouldn't have been so foolish as to do what I did next.

As more attackers ran in, some with superpowers flaring, I charged out to meet them. There was no way I could compete, I knew that. But that didn't matter. This was my fight as much as anyone else's.

It wasn't only that, though. Something else was flowing through me, an inexplicable power, a drive to push myself to the limits. Like the pump you get when you're at the gym, or after you've just slammed someone to the mat in MMA, this was an exhilarating dance of my fists and legs. When I took down the third shooter, I snatched his rifle out of the air before it hit the deck, then spun around and took out two more.

A super came flying at me with an orange light forming at her fists. I shot her in the fucking face, then Navani was at my side, sending two more shots into the super's chest. She gave me a nod of appreciation and a look of surprise, and that fueled me even more.

It was like a bear had woken from its slumber, and now all of these fuckers were trying to take that bear's first meal. With a roar, I ran at a super with a jump kick, feeling unstoppable.

Until that super threw up his hands and an invisible wall slammed into me. My leg hurt like hell, my head cracked against the floor as I fell, and for a moment I lay there, dazed. Navani and Sakurai were fighting around me, the bartender and a couple of others finally joining in. I lifted my head, shaking it, trying to get rid of the ringing.

What the hell had I been thinking, running up on a super like that?

I rolled aside to avoid getting hit by a wave of debris, pushed by a blast of energy that left a line of cracked floor in its wake. The attack hit Sakurai, and I was up again, not about to lay around while she got hurt. Was she more powerful than me, able to stand up for herself? Of course. More powerful by a thousand times, most likely. But that didn't negate her need for my help.

At least this time I was a little more clear-headed, more cautious. A super had turned on her and was morphing into some sort of furry creature. Maybe a wolf? I didn't allow for time to find out, instead opting to slam him in the back of the head with my elbow. Next, I snatched him up by his very hairy head and smacked it into the floor with all my might. Judging by the sick popping sound and blood, I'd at least broken his nose.

Out of the corner of my eye, I saw a figure approaching, so I rolled out of the way before a kick nearly got me. A spray of bullets came from another direction, but I was still rolling and managed to get behind the bar.

As I watched, the wood splintered, and a bullet came for me but then stopped. Right there, an inch from my face, it froze.

A glance over revealed the bartender, hand out with thumb and forefinger almost together, as if he were holding the bullet from the other side of the bar, and then he flicked it back and up. It connected with a super as she leaped up to the bar, so that she fell down, nearly on top of me. She landed head first, face right between my legs as I spread them and scooted back to avoid being hit.

Her eyes rolled up, looked at me, and then went blank.

I gave a nod of appreciation to the bartender, then watched as he threw out more shields to protect the sisters. He and Navani were throwing up shields, doing their best to protect us from the onslaught of attacks.

And then, to my horror, a super appeared like a shadow behind the bartender, thrust her hand up and into his back, and then dropped his dying body to the floor. Her arm was covered in blood, her eyes full black when she turned to look at me—but not fast enough, because I'd reacted the moment I saw her appear. As soon as she saw me, I was there with the pistol from the one who'd died at my crotch moments ago. Firing point-blank into one of those black eyes did the trick.

Shadows drifted away from her like a dark mist rising, and she collapsed. Navani darted past, purple energy coming from her as her shield deflected bullets, and she pulled me with her to the sex closet again.

Hand holding mine, she turned to me and said, "Get to Sakurai, get her out of here."

"Me?"

"Do it, I'll draw their attention." She clenched my hand, giving me energy and new confidence. For some reason, she believed in me. After what I'd just done back there, I wasn't so surprised.

"Go time," I said, and together we sprinted out of there. It was like I was back in the Marines, charging a planet to take down a local warlord who'd gotten too powerful. All of that came back to me, only this time it wasn't about putting someone down, but rescuing someone else.

I plowed through two shooters, feeling that strange burst of energy and strength from earlier, amazed at the power of my punches and my ability to dodge theirs. A shot hit me, but it was a regular bullet and simply caused my personal shield to flash blue. Even though I knew the shield wouldn't last forever, seeing that bullet get deflected like that gave me new hope.

This had also, however, finally caught the attention of Goros.

He turned his attack on me, that green beam of lightning. I'd like to say I didn't piss my pants a little, and maybe I didn't, I honestly don't remember. But whenever someone twice your size turns on you and green electricity flows from their hands to fry the flesh off of your bones, it's terrifying.

That was the first and last time a dragon saved me. To be more precise, the dragon of light that Sakurai created with her sword. It flashed over, cutting off the stream of light—not blocking it, but diverting it so that a gaping hole remained where the roof had been, glass and metal falling in on us, and a moment later she was slashing at him.

He was fast though, or so it appeared. He had

either teleported, or one of his supers had pulled him back with a similar power. Three more supers were teleported into the spot he'd been standing, all with swords, all standing their ground against Sakurai's assault.

More were coming in too, though now Navani was drawing much of their attention. Their numbers were simply too many, their power too much for us to handle. She was right, we had to get out of there, now.

A blast came from Navani, and I turned with worry, only to see her standing there, sexy-ass suit hugging her tight little body, with her hands in the air as if she'd just clapped. All around her, enemies lay scattered. Nice.

Doing my part, I sprinted for Sakurai with every intention of getting her out of there. My legs were moving fast again, faster than normal, and I wished I had time to try and figure out why. What had changed in the last couple of minutes to give me such energy?

Maybe it was just my adrenaline taking over, I didn't know. What I did know was that a group of attackers was moving my way again, and Goros was watching me with curiosity. I might as well give him a show, I thought as I threw a punch.

It missed, the super seeming to melt out of my

way and come up behind me with a kick that sent me right into the punch of the next one. His fist hit me upside the head, and I was thrown to my left, ears ringing. Dammit, that wasn't supposed to happen, not to me. I lifted my pistol to fire when one of them kicked my wrist and sent it flying. Another caught me with a punch to the gut, but I rolled with it, taking his arm and kneeling to flip him over me, as good old Marine Corps training had taught me.

"We have to get out of here!" I told Sakurai, and she glanced back from her fighting, long enough to earn her a slight cut on her shoulder.

She cursed, turning to retaliate, and sliced off the guy's head who'd drawn her blood. Before his head even hit the ground, she'd moved on to the other two again, completely disregarding me.

My only option was to clear a path, which seemed fairly doable considering the fact that more had run off to fight Navani, finally seeing that she was the bigger threat here. As much as my energy and confidence were soaring, I had to keep a level head here. As easily as that punch had caught me off guard, it could have been a bullet or a blast of lightning. Apparently, the shields worked against bullets, so there was that at least. But not punches, and probably not certain other types of non-ranged attacks.

Keeping that in mind, I decided to go after the guys with guns. Running in, arms up to block my face in case the shield didn't extend up far enough, I plowed right into their midst and began tearing it up. As soon as I had a pistol again, I was a killing machine, a rough-tough-can't-get-enough devil dog, do or die, mother fuckers! They landed a couple of strikes, sent a couple of bullets up against my shield, but in the end, I sent them all to meet their maker.

As I turned to see the damage I'd done, I froze. Confused. Shocked.

While I'd left a wake of corpses, it hadn't mattered. Goros stood there with his hand on Sakurai's forehead, energy surging on him, circling like a tornado and then, with a blast, it channeled off of him and exploded into her. Navani reached out, shouting as her eyes went blue, but it was too late…

Sakurai vanished in a blast of energy. Vaporized. Her sword clattered to the floor.

And then all eyes were on us. Weapons and superpowers, and what could we do against their forces?

"Run," Navani shouted, sending out another blast that knocked the enemy over. We had no choice, and as much as I hated the word or the act of it, we were left with only that option.

Retreat.

6

W e sprinted out of the bar, me following Navani as shots exploded dirt and glass behind us. Shouts from Goros echoed after us, but Navani was doing something that pushed us fast, pulling me along with my hand in hers again.

Her eyes glowed blue as she glanced around, and from time to time she would thrust out a hand and energy would ripple, the form of the teleporting super or others he'd try to send would appear in a flash but be gone just as fast.

Several supers burst into the air in flight, but we were quickly approaching the edge of the dunes, where there was a steep drop-off on the other side.

"We'll have to jump," Navani said, pulling me along.

My legs had that extra energy thing going for them, but I was still being pulled about like a rag doll. As with this whole fucking mission, I didn't see any options about arguing with her.

We reached the edge, and she leaped down without hesitation. Hell, who was I to question? But when I saw the fall, I yelped, pulling my hand free as my arms flailed wildly. She was there a moment later, guiding me along the wall as she pushed against it, a purple light coming out from her as she seemed to manipulate the power around her. Another question for later.

Finally, we landed in a new part of the city, totally different from where we had just come from. We were darting around white buildings with blue trim as ships flew by overhead, it looked like a cross between a scene from an old science fiction film and a picture of a Greek village I'd once seen in what felt like another life.

"We failed already," I said, leaning against the wall to catch my breath.

"No," Navani said. "We weren't just running randomly. Her direct sister is here, too."

"Wouldn't that be your sister too?"

"They're all half-sisters." She looked up at the ships flying overhead and sighed. "We came for both of them. We'll leave with one."

She held up a hand, waiting while another ship flew by, then signaled and we darted across, two buildings down and one up, before climbing the stairs to the back door of a house. She kicked it in, and there we were, face-to-face with a goddess.

When I say Navani is beautiful, or that Sakurai was gorgeous, that's one thing. And this woman was too, but when I say she was a goddess, I'm not only referring to her beauty. She was tall, slender, with long blonde hair flowing down her back and eyes of gold that stared into my soul.

"Holy hell," I stammered, trying to think of something to say.

She had apparently finished processing that two people had just burst into her home, because she suddenly transformed, golden eyes glowing hot, the power of the sun coming from her as her hair flew out like the wind was tossing it about.

The unintended consequence of this, I at first thought, was that the robe she had on went flying off. But then I saw that she wasn't nude underneath, and was instead wearing a combat suit of black and red, nearly skintight and in spots almost looking like it was actually painted on. At her chin, metal came out, covering part of her neck and jaw, and wings shot out from behind her—black metallic wings with orange tips like razors.

Looking at her I thought two things at once—we were as good as dead, and dammmnnnn she was hot. And yes, there was the whole heat from her fire thing going on too.

"Two seconds to explain yourselves," she said, voice firm, leaving no room for doubt.

"They're after each of us," Navani explained, moving aside and gesturing out through the doorway.

"Us?" Her heat died down slightly, which I took as a good sign. The longer we stood there, the more confident I became. That same sense of strength and speed was building up in my muscles.

Navani motioned to close the door and waited. The woman nodded. Once it was closed, Navani turned, holding out her hands to show we didn't mean trouble, and said, "Sacrada, sister, the time has come."

"Oh, shit," the woman said. "You're with the Citadel."

"What remains of it, in a sense," Navani said. She went on to quickly fill her in on the situation, what had happened with the fall of the Citadel, and how now they had found me with the help of this Hadrian character's ability to create gateways or portals. Then she got to the awkward part. She held her head high, chest out, and said, "And now we have to get you to safety, to fulfill our mission. To bring a god back into this world."

Sacrada scoffed, looked at me, then to her, and scoffed again. She let her fire finally die down, folding her wings back up so that they were part of her suit and not even noticeable. "Tell me you don't actually believe our parents were gods."

"Not actual gods," Navani said with a frown. "But as far as powers go, unrivaled. They might as well have been gods."

"The Ex Gods," Sacrada said, shaking her head. "You know that's what they call us, right? Those of us who could've been gods, who would've stood at the top of society had our parents not up and vanished."

"I don't need to be a god," Navani said.

"And you?" Sacrada turned my way, her eyes flaring up slightly again. As they did so, I felt an urge to do great things.

"You're a god as far as I'm concerned," I said, almost in a daze. "Both of you, I'm—"

"Drew," Navani interrupted, shaking her head.

"I meant, do you fancy yourself the father of a

god," Sacrada explained. "Clearly, you're not at that level of overconfidence yet."

I shrugged. "Just a man, trying to survive. Here to do what needs to be done."

She laughed at that. "And that's all we are to you, tasks that 'need to be done,' is that it?"

"It's not like that," Navani said. "He's being tested, trained. He'll be one of the Elders."

"Based on what? Do you know anything about this man other than who his father supposedly was? For all we know, he's a serial killer back home."

"First of all, what?" I said. "Second, I'm not. For the record. I have no record, other than assault from this time I beat the shit out of a guy for smacking around his girl. When she wouldn't press charges, the two pointed the finger my way and... You don't care, do you?"

"An Elder, Navani explained to me. "If all of this goes as planned, you will join the forces of the Citadel, possibly earn your rank as one of the supers responsible for protecting its ancient power."

"Huh." It was a bit much to process.

She took that as a sign for more. "Basically, it harnesses the powers of the sun, those same powers that made us supers, and allows us to be... more super."

"The point remains that she doesn't know a

damn thing about you," Sacrada butted in, "and she's not only ready to let you try to impregnate all of us, including my sister and me, but also train to become one of the sacred protectors of our worlds?"

"Er…" I turned to Navani, who was pursing her lips, eyeing the other woman.

"I know enough," she finally countered. "I know he's put himself on the line, risked his life trying to fight for us, and came along without putting up too much of an argument. And… and he opened a door for the lady at the bank, I saw that and how he threw himself in front of Eclypse's attack."

"No shit?" Sacrada raised a perfect, golden eyebrow. "Did you put your pussy on the table before or after you asked him to come along?"

"This is pointless," I cut in. "Maybe we tell her what happened," I said to Navani, "then give her a choice. It's not like we're going to force her, and you certainly won't convince her like this. Meanwhile, the enemy is out there, and for all we know they'll start bombing the city at any minute."

"What…happened?" Sacrada asked, eyeing me and then Navani.

Navani went right out with it. "We tried to save Sakurai, but he got to her."

"Who?" Sacrada asked, eyes flaring up again and a gold mist forming around her head.

"He sent Goros after us, and Goros is the one who did it."

Sacrada turned, took a deep breath, and let the fire die down as a circle of light formed from her head, shooting out. A moment later, the light returned, like radar or sonar.

"Fuck me," she said, then eyed me and said, "and no, that wasn't an invitation."

I didn't think that was fair, considering it was Navani who was telling me I had to screw everyone, but I kept my mouth shut.

"What is it?" Navani asked. "What did you see?"

"So many enemies..." Sacrada cursed again, licked her lips, and turned our way. "And what, now Goros is going to come after me?"

"He plans to kill all of the sisters, as well as Drew and his brother. That's the plan, to ensure Ranger's unchallenged reign."

"And Ranger has already taken down the Citadel and the Elders?"

"As I've explained, it's complicated. But... pretty much."

She nodded. "Then my best chance of getting revenge is to come with you while we search out the other sisters, and use that as a sort of bait for Goros."

"As long as you come with us, I'd say yes, killing

Goros will be part of the plan," Navani smiled and stuck out a hand. "Welcome to the team."

Sacrada scrunched her nose at the hand, shook her head, and then pointed at me. "And I'm not making sweet love to baldy over there, no matter how rugged and handsome he is. It's the principle of the thing."

Navani was clearly bothered by the statement, but she nodded. "Just, keep an open mind."

"How's this for open?" Sacrada looked her up and down, and smiled. "I'd sooner fuck you."

Both Navani and I stared, open-mouthed, at that. Not that it was rare for women to be into women, but it just hadn't been what we'd been expecting. The look on Navani's face showed she wasn't so sure about this situation anymore, which made me laugh.

There wasn't any time or reason to discuss it any further though, so we made our move. Navani's eyes flared, and she told us to wait, but Sacrada sent out her circles of light, and they bounced back a moment later.

"We can handle them," she said and charged out through the front door as a group of supervillains was moving down the street. Here I got to see the powers of Sacrada, and the hint that she wasn't into guys was a real downer, because I wanted her more than ever after seeing her in action.

As they started pulling guns and knives, one lifting his hands and sending nearby rocks and other debris into the air, she swung up, wings extending, and swooped down to them. Sunbursts shot out, enemies burnt to ash instantly. I could feel the heat from here.

When the rocks started to fly at her, she spun, blades on her wings cutting down the man with those powers.

Navani held a finger to her collar and said, "Lamb, we're going to need a ride out of here. Scanning for location now." As the fighting continued below, she held out a hand to an area beyond the houses, and a blue line of light flashed before vanishing. "Set."

"I'll be there shortly," Lamb replied through the comms.

A super wearing a dragon-shaped helmet swept down behind me, his arms also looking like the wings of a dragon. He wore battle armor, unlike many of the others, so I assumed he was higher ranked.

"Navani," I said, moving away.

But with that step, I realized I still had the feeling in me, the hype as I decided to call it, and I decided to try this guy on. He pulled out some sort of blaster from his side, one that I doubted my shield would handle.

I leaped to the side but overdid it, not yet knowing my strength and speed, so that I went flying right into some other guy who'd thought to attack me at that moment. I grabbed him though, pulling him with me so that we fell to the ground. The next blast came our way, but I had this guy up, and he got hit, not me.

Then I charged, holding up this guy as a shield, and slammed him into the dragon-wannabe. It was enough to knock the blaster free, and as I grabbed him by the helmet and yanked, a swooshing sounded overhead announcing the arrival of Lamb with our ship.

Navani was using her purple matter to throw up energy shields that hovered before us. Next, she thrust her hand out, and the purple created a blast wave that knocked over opponents.

"Get to the ship!" she shouted.

The super with the ability to teleport appeared, then was gone only to reappear with a woman at his side. Sacrada turned as the woman shot out a blast of ice, and the angel of a woman fell back, fire flickering. She growled, and the sunbursts shot out, but the teleporter and his girlfriend had now vanished, only to reappear on the other side to strike again.

They weren't paying attention to me though, so on their next teleport, I leaped. When I landed on the woman, I grabbed her and fell, instantly wanting to die. It was like I'd been turned to ice throughout. But as the woman turned on me, I pushed through it, finding a surge of power coming and then, to my surprise, my fist rained down on her with a flurry of blue and ice shot out, surrounding her.

A burst of sun flare took the teleporter, though I wasn't sure if he'd been scorched out of existence or escaped, as the only sign of him left was the blackened dirt. I had to assume the latter, but right now we needed to move.

I reached out a hand for Sacrada to take, but she stared at it. My hand was ice blue, though it felt normal. In fact, my whole body felt fine.

"Get to the ship," she said, and then Navani was there at my side, eyeing me with curiosity as we ran. We darted past the buildings and hit the designated landing spot as shots went off all around us, the enemy ships having now learned where we were. Lamb had the ramp open and was already returning fire as we darted in.

We made it, a rumbling started, and we took off. The three of us did our best to balance and run along the passage to the bridge when a scream sounded. It seemed to be coming from Sacrada's head, even though her mouth wasn't moving. She fell to her knees, covering her ears, and now her scream joined the other.

"What's happening to her?" I shouted.

Navani stood over us, an anxious expression on her face as she turned back to the bridge.

"Bring her. Hurry."

I wrapped an arm around Sacrada, heaving her up and pulling her along in spite of her thrashing. We reached the bridge shortly after Navani, and she had already pulled up the display. There was Goros, and somehow, inexplicably, there was Sakurai. They were on a ship too, and I guessed they were in pursuit.

"Looks like you lost something," Goros said, his face twisting in evil glee.

"I thought you'd want to see this," Lamb said turning to Navani with a look of sorrow.

"One down, three to go," Goros said. "Although, I've always been a gambling man. Double or nothing, eh?"

"Spit it out," Navani said, stepping toward the screen. "We're not here to play games."

"We both know where you're going, and we know I'm coming too." Goros pulled Sakurai close.

She sort of vanished and then reappeared, as if she were an image flickering in and out. "She can't escape, and I imagine you'll want your chance to save her. Fine, let's find out what happens when you're pitted against me in all-out war. We land, you take your time, prepare, whatever you need to do before dying, then come and try to get her."

I glanced over at Sacrada, who stood staring at the screen in pure hatred.

"Where?" Navani asked.

"You're going to Arolla, if my intel serves me right?"

Navani glanced back, trying to hide her shock and worry. I had a good guess what that meant. If they already knew where we were going, they likely had people there waiting. But there was no use denying it.

"I see by your reaction that the intel is accurate," he said, smile fading to a look of determination. "Let's make this fun, shall we? The old ruins, just outside of Demekal. They're already in shambles— let's finish the job while killing each other off. Deal?"

"You're sick," Navani said.

"How do we know you won't just kill her on the way?" Sacrada cut in, voice low, harsh.

"Because, my angel, that would ruin the fun." He made a swiping motion, and an image appeared on the screen, projected in front of his head. At first glance, I thought it was some ancient, alien symbol, and then I realized it was a map. An insane one, at that. And…a maze. "Your sister will be in the center, shown via display over our heads so that you know she's safe. But don't keep your eye on the prize for too long, or one of my supers will gut you. I'd prefer to save that job for myself."

"Fuck you," Sacrada said.

"If you'd prefer, we can do that first." He gave her a wicked grin, and then the screen went blank.

Nobody spoke for a very, very long moment. We braced ourselves, strapped in, and exited atmosphere before anyone said another word. Finally, when artificial gravity had kicked in, and we were on our way, Sacrada stood and turned to us with a glare.

"Did you see a body?" Sacrada asked.

I shook my head. "But we saw her—"

"Explode?" Sacrada kicked at the air, then turned on me, eyes blazing gold. "That's what she does! She controls matter, pulling a sword from nearby metal is her trademark move, as you might have seen, and the tattoos help her pull forces similar to familiars. But in a moment of near death, she's able to sort of reset herself, not really traveling through time, but reconstructing herself to where she was a minute prior. It can come in real handy, but she has limitations on how often she can use it. Too soon after the previous time and we believe she wouldn't be able to come back. Certain powers limit that ability, restrain her…"

"So she did this, only to be caught again, this time without us there to help," Navani said. "Well, don't we feel like big dicks."

"Where's their ship?" Sacrada asked. "We're going after her, now."

"Their fleet, you mean? Lamb, would you…" Navani gestured to the screen as Lamb pulled up an image of the ships we'd seen before, plus a very large one flying at their center. They all had that crazy look of exploded metal blown back, razor-like wings. "We'd be dead before we came within eyesight."

Sacrada glared at us, then back to the now blank screen. She took a deep breath. "It's not your fault," she said, and then stood and walked out.

"Damn," I said. "If I'd thought there was a chance, I never would have left."

"I know." Navani frowned. "Something tells me we won't be starting on our *mission* any time soon."

It didn't seem like the best time to be thinking about something like sex, but I had to remind myself that, to her, it wasn't just about getting laid with multiple hot women. The act served a larger purpose, one with dire consequences if not fulfilled.

"Sometimes," I started, not sure how to word this. "Sometimes sex can be more than just physical pleasure, or even baby making."

She looked at me with pursed lips, like she wasn't sure if she should laugh or not. Whatever, I didn't care. This needed to be dealt with.

"What I'm saying is, we're all stressed. We don't really know if we can trust each other yet, or at least feel completely comfortable. You know?"

"Drew?" She smiled, at least. "Is this really the way you're going to try to work up to us fucking?"

"Is it supposed to be this difficult?"

She laughed—not a joyful laugh, but an ironic one. "No, I don't think so." For a moment she looked outside, watching space go by, then said, "Lamb, you got the controls? I put in the destination. We have to be sure we beat Goros there."

"Roger that," Lamb said, appearing at her side. She grinned at me. "Something in mind?"

"Actually, yes," Navani said. She unstrapped, then stood and reached for my hand. "Drew here is going to try and seduce me. And I might just let him."

I gulped as I unstrapped and accepted. Her hand was warm, welcoming. Both women's eyes moved down to the raging boner I hadn't even realized popped up, so I quickly tucked it away.

"Ah, the soldier's excited," Navani said with a chuckle. "Don't worry, he'll be coming out to play soon enough."

I couldn't believe this was happening. As we walked out, I felt a pat on my ass and looked back to see Lamb give me a wink before vanishing. If only she were real, or alive, or whatever the situation was with her. Having her in the mix certainly would've been welcome.

7

The viewing deck was peaceful, and my outfit had transformed into a bathrobe for me. It was hard to focus with everything going on, and I felt horrible for Sacrada and her sister. Yet, here was this beautiful woman in front of me, biting gently on her lip and ready to fuck. If I'd learned anything about sex in my life, it was that intimate acts not only helped bring people together but served as great stress relievers.

"Lamb, please give us privacy here," Navani said, taking me by the lapels of my bathrobe and pulling me close.

"But you said, you didn't want this to get too personal—" Lamb argued, cut off by Navani clearing her throat. "Roger that. Getting out of your way."

"The first time I met her, I was still aspiring to enter the Citadel," Navani said, eyes lingering on the spot Lamb had just vanished from. "Still a student at the academy, looking up to this legendary woman. I never would've thought I'd be hanging a sock on the bedroom door to keep her out, if you know what I mean."

I grinned. "We have that saying on Earth, too. So yes."

"Is it weird that I wanted to be her? Like, I mean I drew a bit, and made a poster of her and put it on my wall. I might have even, I don't know, wondered about myself while looking at that poster from time to time. Not that I have any doubts now, though," she quickly added with a glance at my crotch."

"We're about to… you know. How is you being curious weird?" I thought about it, then added, "Then again, can't she hear you? That part might be a bit awkward."

She laughed, nervously. "As far as I know, when she agrees to give us privacy, she does."

"So if you wanted to kill me right now…"

"Totally could." She stepped closer, hand held out as if debating whether to reach for me. "Although that would defeat the purpose of bringing you here, I'm not really sure you can handle what I'm about to bring. You might die of excitement. Heart failure?"

"Wow, think highly of yourself, do you?"

She shrugged. "I worked hard to look this good, but I'm the kind of woman who knows it's not only about the looks."

My mouth went dry as she finally stepped closer, fingers tracing a line from my chest to my abs.

"Are you sure about this?" I asked.

"It's my duty," she said.

I pulled back. "Can we word it differently?"

"How would you have me word it?"

"Well, I'll be honest." I stepped forward, so that her hand moved into my robe, caressing my bare chest. "Since the moment I saw you, I've wanted you. We're here to make a super baby, and that might freak me out a bit... and I'm all about mission accomplishment. Marine, remember? But for me, this is so much more." I traced the contours of her armor, up along the edge of her breast, and noticed that she shuddered, eyes taking me in with hunger now. "Can you feel that?"

She nodded. "Sensors. Turned off for pain, but on else wise."

"Really?" I grinned, running my hand along her back, tracing her hip bone back to the front. She looked up at me, those blue eyes going almost white on the edges, almost normal. There was a look of hope there, of desire, even. My hand moved down, caressing the hard metal between her legs.

She moaned, eyes closing in the moment, and then she tore off my robe, grabbed my cock, and gave me a challenging look. "You were saying, about it being more?"

With a heavy breath, I leaned in and kissed her. Her lips quivered, pressing back slightly, and then she was stroking me, slow and gentle as if my cock was the most precious thing she'd ever held.

She nibbled on my lip and then reached back, lowering herself to the ground, and took my hand to lower me too. Her armor was still on, but she waved a hand over a sensor on her forearm, entered a code, and it folded off of her until it was liquid metal, sliding off to the sides and out of the way.

"Biotech armor," she said, watching as my eyes roamed over her body. I wasn't bothering to hide that I liked what I saw. Breasts that, while not perky since she was on her back, still held their form, abs that were tight from exercise, and a cute little landing strip over her pussy.

She noticed my eyes lingering there, the smile on my lips, and said, "I knew about the mission, so... figured I'd make it count." She motioned me forward with a finger.

I knelt, moving over to her, and lowered myself

down on top of her. "You know, it's somehow less awkward now that we're about to do it."

"It was until you spoke," she said with a laugh. Her hand found my cock again, and she held it, moving to look at it, and then closed her eyes and wrapped her legs around my back.

Gently now, she guided me in. Her skin was smooth, her pussy wet. The head of my cock slid in, feeling the pressure, resistance, and she arched her back. No foreplay, I guess, when the point is to get going. Then again, she'd been so wet, I supposed it didn't matter as much. Still, for me a bit of buildup had always helped my erections be as strong as possible, so I continued the slow movement while I grabbed her ass, ran my hand along her thighs and between, feeling the sides of her pussy, the base of my cock, and then I lifted her so that I was holding her while I knelt, lifting her up and down as I worked my tongue around her breast, sucked the nipple, and then laid back so that she was riding me.

She stopped, staring past me, and I rotated to get a glimpse of what had caused her to freeze. I'd have expected Goros to be there, but it was only Sacrada. She glared, mouth open in shock, and then rolled her golden eyes.

"Sacrada," Navani said as the woman started to turn.

"Is this really the best time?" Sacrada said, spinning on us. "I thought my sister was dead, now I've learned she's in the hands of one of the most ruthless supervillains alive. And you two... you two are fucking!"

She stormed off, but when she reached the stairs, Navani called after her, "It's the mission."

"What mission?" she spat back.

"*The* mission," Navani said, then gestured down to my nude form. Slowly, she started riding me again, eyeing the other woman.

Sacrada watched, eyes widening, and then put her hand to her mouth. "Oh, shit. I thought that was a bunch of B.S. You're for real?"

Navani sat on me, dick still inside of her, and stared at the woman. "Excuse me? B.S.? How else do you propose we make a move against the evil if not with an heir?"

"Wow, dude," she looked at me and scoffed, "you've found yourself one of the crazies. Just as long as you know that."

I frowned, looking back to Navani, who shook her head and said, in a kind of crazy way, "No, not crazy. Maybe crazy about cranberry walnut bread, but not crazy in general. Could you imagine some cranberry walnut bread right now?"

Oddly enough, she wasn't the first woman to

ever bring up cranberry walnut bread with me during sex.

"You're a religious fanatic," Sacred said to her. "Listen to yourself, or hell, look at yourself. You're having sex with a man you barely know, simply because some legend says our DNA and his can create a superpowerful ultra-super?"

"How dare you?" Navani said, standing so that my dick flopped back onto my belly. Unfinished, I thought with a sigh.

"Oh, fuck," Sacrada said, eyes narrowing. "You came after my sister and me, for this? For this?!"

"We have to try!" Navani shouted.

"Ladies, can we jus—"

"SHUT UP!" They both turned on me, glaring with eyes that dared me to say another word.

"How does a baby help save us anyway?" Sacrada asked after a second, with a mixture of annoyance and actual curiosity.

"According to research we've been able to pull and intel, thanks to the Citadel and the Elders, bless them," Navani lowered her head for a moment of silence, "the true enemy isn't easily accessible. It's not a baby that will save us, but what the baby will grow into. He will attend the best superhero school, but will be sheltered so that the enemy cannot trace him. In the meantime, once we defeat Ranger, we will be able to send a ship of our best out to this galaxy, including Hadrian's essence, stored just for this. He will use the last of his powers to create the final gateway."

"And you'll send the baby through?" I asked, very confused now.

"Even with FTL and jumps in place, the travel is expected to take up to twenty years," she explained. "Hadrian creates gates back to locations he's been, but can never create one to a location he hasn't visited. Once we've arrived, we open the gate and send the young man we have hopefully helped create through this gateway, along with the best supers we can find, and we finish this war."

"Talk about a long game," Sacrada said, shaking her head. "Count on the Citadel to come up with something this insane."

"It's that or be conquered, ultimately destroyed," Navani argued. "You have a better plan?"

A long silence followed, during which my head started pounding as I tried to grasp the magnitude of what I was involved in.

"And for the record," Sacrada turned her head, flipping gold curls out of her face, "you and me, guy? Never going to happen."

She descended the stairs, leaving me to stare at Navani's perfect ass. After a moment she turned, growled, and the blue in her eyes was back. As I started to get back up, she put her foot on my shoulder and pushed me back down.

"Where do you think you're going?" she asked.

"Um, aren't we done?"

She laughed, an almost mean one, then straddled me and leaned in close, hands grabbing my face. "Fuck that. We're putting a baby in me to prove her wrong."

Then she rolled us over. This time I didn't need her to guide me in—her legs were spread and pussy moist. A new side of her was emerging, one that had no problem screaming, "Fuck me, fuck me, fuck me!" and running her hands along my back, slapping my ass, and, at one point, turning over doggy style while sucking my finger that she pulled up to her mouth. Her ass felt so good slapping against my legs, balls swinging as I went to town on her. I reached out and took her purple hair and grabbed hold, pulling slightly to see if she was into it. She yelped, growled, and then starting moving her hips against mine even harder.

Finally, I spasmed, almost falling on her as my chest muscles clenched and a warmth passed through my body. Each breath came heavier while she was yelling for me to come, shouting to do it, fill her with my seed, and I was stuck somewhere between trying not to laugh at the use of the word seed again, and giving myself over to the complete bliss that was this sensation of her pussy on my dick.

I leaned back to see it, to rub my hand down her ass cheek and along her asshole, and then I grabbed those ass cheeks as my orgasm took over. Thrusts came in jolts now, her pussy clenching and unclenching around my cock, and then I was spent, and she was leaning down. Moaning.

Instead of just lying next to her, I reached up and ran my hand along her thigh. Playing with the curve of her ass, I moved my hand slowly down to hold her pussy, then spread my fingers along the edges before moving back up to find her clit, massaging it. Her body trembled, and she let out a low whimper.

"Is that a good sound, or…?" I started to ask, but she simply glanced over at me, closed her eyes, and moaned one long, pleasure-filled moment.

"Good," she whispered. "Very good."

She turned over, hips in the air, giving me a view I would've gladly paid for mere minutes before.

"Stop staring, perv," she said. "I'm trying to get your seed to settle."

"Ahhh." I turned onto my side, watching her face instead. A look of determination, but she wouldn't turn my way. Finally, she lowered her hips, rubbed her stomach just below the belly button, and nodded.

She reached out toward the liquid metal, and it came to her, surrounding her, clothing her. This time, it took on the shape of a Japanese robe, a yukata. She stood, and without another word headed for stairs.

"Really, just like that?" I asked.

She paused, clutched the yukata tight, and then kept going.

"At least it's not awkward anymore," I called out to her, but she glanced back, frowned, and then walked off.

How was it possible to feel so good, and at the same time so bad?

I stood, found my robe—as I didn't know how to do the fancy liquid metal trick yet, and put it on. Not knowing what to do with myself, I wandered the viewing deck, looking at the stars, wondering how I was going to navigate this crazy galaxy.

For no reason that I could explain, I had a sudden urge to run and jump. To practice the kicks and punches I'd learned in the Marines, and so I did. Each leap was like someone had thrown me, and I had to assume it was related to the ship's gravity. But then I would land with a boom when I wanted to. I punched the air and felt my fists moving faster than made sense, faster than seemed humanly possible.

I stared at my hands, taking a break, sweat dripping down my chest. They seemed to be glowing slightly, red, and I had the urge to try something. Pulling back, I prepared with a deep breath, then threw my body into a punch and nearly fell back with surprise as red energy formed around my fist and exploded in the spot I'd stopped the strike. Either I was becoming one of them, or had been all along, and now it was coming to life, like a dragon left dormant, now waking to unleash hell.

I didn't know whether to laugh with joy or curl up in a ball of dread. It was too much for my mind to handle, so I closed my eyes, took a deep breath… and the feeling faded.

When I opened my eyes, an aftershock went through me in the form of a chill, and I breathed out, remembering how it had felt to cum inside of her. As bad as this place might get, that pretty much made up for it.

8

Figuring I'd pondered life long enough, and wanting answers regarding my display of powers a few moments before, I started to leave the viewing room. However, when I reached the stairs, Lamb appeared in front of me, smiling with her hands folded before her.

"You fought back there, on the planet?" she asked.

I nodded.

"Then you must want to check your stats," she said. "See if you are close to leveling up."

"Close to… what?"

She smiled, then started to walk around me, looking me over. "You are quite the man, aren't you?"

"I don't know how to answer that."

She shrugged. "At any rate, you're about to become even more of one. I think for you, tank skill trees will be appropriate. Let's see…" With a wave of her hand, a screen appeared before me. It had an image of me, but then several descriptions of attack and defense skills that were all way over my head.

"I don't understand," I admitted.

"You will," she promised. "Not all of the others will see it the same. Your brother, for instance, has special powers that relate to mixing with supers, in a sense."

"Right, because he's supposedly a super too…" I shook my head, trying to get the dull ache out of it. "How do you know all this?"

"Let's just say we're connected. You, him, Navani. Others… and once that's happened, I can see a great deal about you. My powers work in a sort of leveling up way, enhancing the abilities that are already there, within you. But they are limited, which is why we have to focus on strengths for you. As you gain more power, it opens up and fuels my power, like adding more wood to a fire."

The Marine in me wanted to make a joke about putting my wood in her fire, but the nervous side of me won out, and instead, I simply said, "Well, shit."

She smiled. "Shit indeed. Let's have a look." In a flash, she was at my side, looking at my screen.

"Nobody else can see this, by the way. Only you and, while I'm around, me." She moved her hand and the screen swiped up, replaced by lines of code. She frowned. "There are others better at reading this, but… I'll be damned, this is interesting."

"Great! Mind filling me in on what the hell is happening?"

She pointed to a line as if I would understand. "I think this is telling me how your powers work. Not like your brother's at all, but… yes, very interesting indeed. It looks like you can absorb the energy around you. Not steal it, but grow with it, sort of like a bloodlust."

"Me?"

"I wouldn't even have seen it if…" She stopped, laughed, and then turned to me. "Want to know why it's spiked just now?" When she saw I was staring at her, confused and dumbfounded, she went on. "Basically, it's like you get more power when you're close to someone, but it goes through the roof with intimate activities. Maybe it's fueled by your hormones, I don't know, but it's interesting as hell. That's why I was starting to say, I wouldn't even have seen it if you two hadn't just gotten freaky."

"Which explains what happened just now," I said, thinking back to my jumping and punching, and the way that red energy had formed with my strike. "Wait. I thought she told you to give us privacy."

"It's hard when you're part of the ship, part of you both, in a sense."

"I don't know what that means, exactly," I admitted. "But what you're saying is, if I have sex with a super, I become more... super?"

She grinned. "Intimacy. Yes. That doesn't have to be sex, of course. You've probably even gained small amounts of powers back on Earth when you kissed a woman. Did you ever feel an extra charge, I mean more than other men would have?"

"How would I know?"

"Ah, right." She frowned, then shrugged. "Point being, with a super, you'll feel it. Even being close to one will help, but you get a kiss before you punch someone? Bam. You get a hand job or..." She paused to gesture sucking a dick, and I felt my cock move with excitement. Too bad she was a ghost, kinda. "Well, you get the idea. And according to this, it charges up, too."

"Like, the more intimate I get, not only will the powers be stronger, but they'll last longer?"

"Exactly. See, you're not as dumb as she says you are."

"The fuck?"

"Oh, I mean," she winked, "got you."

"Not funny." I clenched my jaw, more annoyed that I was bothered by her saying it than by the fact that she had said it. Growing up, Chad had always been the smart one, while I was the tough guy, the jock. The Marine, now.

After a moment of watching me, she turned back to the screen, flipping it back to the branching. "Anyway... see here."

"What am I looking at?"

"This is your skill tree. Like in games, though I see that doesn't mean much to you," she laughed. "Here you have options. When you want to pull up the screen, just will it. The suit knows how, it's adaptable and reacts to the signals your body emits. Fancy? You're welcome."

"Thanks." I was still waiting.

"Ah, right. So, the skill trees let you upgrade. I've set it up for you and the other supers from Earth—those of you who will, we hope, become Elders—so that it resembles what you're used to. Little did I know some of you are super-jocks who don't know this shit." With a roll of her eyes, she motioned to a number at the top right of the screen, then the first two options. "You're easy, so we've set you up like a tank. Basically, attack or defense. Ranged attack is included, by the way."

I looked at the tiers, starting to get the hang of it.

As I watched, a shield appeared over one, a knife over the other.

"There, that should help," she said with a wink."

"Thanks. So I have one skill point now," I said. "Do I get to use that wherever?"

"Pick the one you want. You'll get more skill as you absorb power, fight, teach your body and the suit how to adapt and be better. Harder opponents mean you've challenged yourself, so naturally it will grow with you. It's not by its nature as much like a game, but…we've made it more so."

"To make it easier, yeah, I get that." I laughed. Easier my ass. "Here I thought I just got to come along for the ride, bang some hot chicks, and get back to my life."

Her expression looked horrified. "Is that all this is to you?"

"No…?"

She made a tsk-tsk sound, looked at me sadly, and said, "Let's get this over with then, so you can go back to banging hot chicks and not giving a fuck."

"That's harsh," I said. "I care. You think I want to be here?" As soon as the words left my mouth, I realized that, yeah, of course I did. Shit, what was left for me back home?

She saw it in my eyes and simply scoffed.

"But, no," I protested. "Look, what do you want

from me? I'm out of my league here. I have no idea what's really going on. For all I know, I've been abducted by crazy people like Sacrada says!"

"Is it crazy to give my life for the cause?" she said, appearing an inch away from my face.

"Depending on the cause, yes," I countered.

"Considering the fact we're talking about not only our galaxy being taken over by a bunch of supervillains who'd see everyone tortured, those without powers—and even those with lesser powers —enslaved… I'd say it's a pretty damn good cause. I'd happily sacrifice myself again if it means we have a chance of stopping them. I would have thought a *Marine* would understand this."

As often happened, I was being an insensitive blockhead. You don't go around telling people who have died for their cause, in a sense, that you're not convinced they gave their life for the right reason. If everything they said was true, of course I had to step up.

Most of all, I needed to remember that I was right there with them in this. What good did it do to question any of it? Either I did my duty, with my cock and my fists, or it would be better to just leave it all behind.

So I committed.

"I'm all in," I said. "No more of this bullshit. And

you know what? I'm going to own it, own my being a jackass. I'm sorry."

She blinked, looked around, and said, "Shit."

"What?"

"I just… supers where I'm from, especially the males, rarely apologize." She grinned, nodding with respect. "You're more man than I thought."

"That's all it takes?"

"Hey, for some guys, that's a lot." She looked me up and down, then said, "Too bad I'm not a real being. I mean in the flesh and all that. I'd go down on you right now, I'm so turned on. If it's possible to be turned on in my state… it's confusing."

"Well, thank you." I shifted, uncomfortably.

"Shields!" she exclaimed, likely trying to get her mind back on track.

"What?"

She avoided my eye contact, pointing at the screen. "For shields, you'll be able to upgrade to all sorts of elemental resistance, even upgrades that send an attack back at your enemy when they hit you, but on the first level it's really about increasing the power your shield can take and the recharge rate."

"And this shield, it's part of my current outfit?"

She nodded, glanced down, and laughed. I looked to see my cock was showing, sticking up again, of

Title:	Supers: Ex Gods
Cond:	Good
User:	marissav_list
Station:	DESKTOP-8SELUVJ
Date:	2024-12-03 15:23:42 (UTC)
Account:	Blue Vase Books
Orig Loc:	Aisle 20-Bay 7-Shelf 9
mSKU:	BVM.JLN
vSKU:	BVV.1717538622.G
Seq#:	1006
unit_id:	23186083
width:	0.79 in
rank:	4,276,949
Cond Note:	The item shows wear from consistent use, but it remains in good condition and works perfectly. All pages and cover are intact (including the dust cover, if applicable). Spine may show signs of wear. Pages may include limited notes and highlighting. May NOT include access code or other

course. Apparently, even though the conversation had moved on from the topic of her going down on me, he hadn't.

"You can change it with your thoughts," she said. "The outfit, that is. Visually, if you prefer, but it's not necessary."

The screen of outfits popped up like earlier, and I picked the Marine outfit with battle armor.

"And attacks?"

She selected the knife on the screen now. "Mostly, due to the nature of your powers, you'll be getting increases to damage, stun attacks, stuff like that in the early tiers." Scrolling across, she showed me a few of the lower tiers, all grayed out, as they weren't available. "As you can see, there are some pretty cool options as you progress in the skill tree."

She wasn't lying. While some were simply upgrades to damage dealt, other options included a berserker mode, stun attack, and even an explosive attack. I could already imagine myself punching Goros in the head and seeing that thing pop like a watermelon.

"Wherever you want to use the skill, just touch it, and it'll go through," she explained.

I frowned, lifted my finger, and debated. Who was I kidding, though? I'd always been more of a charge in and take the hill kind of guy. The first attack skill was one that said it increased damage with the number of hits landed in a row, without interruption. I liked the sound of that! Selecting it, the image lit up, the line to it as well. It was part of my skill tree.

"Man, I can't wait to try that," I said, pumped up and ready for action.

"You can go ahead," Lamb said. "We will jump soon, when we've reached the next gate. Hadrian has certain ones already set up, only accessible to those who know where they are. We'll be using one that's about an hour away. Until then, hit up the dojo, see what you can do."

She didn't have to tell me twice, and when she showed me how to pull up a mini-map on my screen and highlighted the dojo, I thanked her before jogging off to kick some punching bag ass.

9

A voice in the back of my head said I should be checking in on Navani, but she was the one who wanted to keep it impersonal. If anything, I'd been used. Well, fuck it. I didn't mind. And I assumed she wanted a break by the way she'd simply stood up and left when we were done.

Either way, I kinda needed another form of release. I liked to think that I could fuck and be totally emotionally detached, but it just wasn't me. Was I a tough guy? A Marine who had done my share of killing, and now, as it turned out, was destined to be some great Elder of the superheroes? You bet your tiny ass. I was a badass. But.

It's always been that way for me. It's not like I needed her to stare into my eyes and say she loved me—that would have turned me off instantly, I was sure. But the moment a woman's hand was on my dick, it was like she'd reached into my soul, been one with me. Become part of my life, even if we never spoke again.

Of course, if anyone ever told that to my old Marine buddies, I'd cut off said person's dick and shove it so far up their nostrils they'd be fucking their own brains. Just saying.

Point is, I needed another form of release.

I stepped into the dojo, ready to tear a punching bag the fuck open. And then I stood there, confused. It was a large, empty room. Pure white, but with a metallic gleam.

"Um… Lamb?"

"Yes," she said, not appearing.

"I wanted to punch something."

"Then you're in the right place. Step forward and say so."

"Okay." I frowned, but stepped forward and said, "Give me something to punch."

Lights dimmed, then flashed out. When they came back on again, I was surrounded by humanoids—not living, I realized as they started moving for me, but liquid metal hardening as they approached. They moved just like humans, only faster. Like supers.

"Welcome to the simulation dojo," Lamb said. "If it gets to be too much, use the safety word."

"Ah, right. What safety word would that be?"

A laugh echoed throughout the dojo, and she said, "Good luck," voice fading.

"Excuse me? Lamb? Lamb?"

But she wasn't answering, and the robots were closing in on me. Well, not robots I guess, but that was the closest way I could comprehend them.

"Let's see what you've got," I said, preparing to take them down as I had the supervillains.

They came at me at once, all of them, surrounding me and throwing a barrage of strikes that were sure to leave me battered and bruised. I tried to dodge a strike, got slammed in the forehead. Bobbed and weaved, took a shot in the gut. When I went for a takedown, one of them connected its knee with my jaw, and I fell, hard.

Luckily for me, they all backed off. Apparently, this wasn't a "kill Drew" simulation. With a deep breath, I pushed myself up and ran at the closest one. My side-kick actually caught it, sending it sprawling backward. I ducked immediately and took a step back, only to find a robot had moved with me and came in for an arm lock. Damn, that hurt.

At least I was being challenged.

I managed to roll out of it, then spun and landed

a punch—good thing the metal wasn't actual metal, too! My fist hit, and the robot's face gave way slightly, feeling somewhat like a silicon job this girl I used to date had. Talk about hard-ass titties! I still had my fun with them, and they never hit me back, unlike these guys.

That shot cost me my position, and I was overexposed. Three good hits from surrounding robots dropped me, and again I had to lie there, taking deep breaths. Something wasn't working here, and I had to adjust.

It had been too long since I'd had sex, I realized. Whatever bonus I'd gotten from that was gone. But I was still a fighter, I still had my recent upgrade. Problem was, I needed to land a couple of punches in a row before that would matter.

Which meant I had to think smarter.

I stopped going for power strikes, instead focusing on quick dodges and weaves, jabbing with my left, moving around them, and backing myself into a corner so they couldn't surround me. So much of this was the opposite of what I'd normally do in a fight, but with so many opponents and with my specific power, it totally worked.

When I landed my fourth strike in a row, I realized I was already punching harder, and probably had been since the second. My fifth, for example, was barely a hook to one of the robot's midsections, but it sent it stumbling back as if I'd landed a roundhouse kick to it. One of the other robots landed a kick on my thigh, breaking the combo, but I used the moment to strike back, get out of dodge, and then quickly catch him twice in the back.

Since one was recovering and this one fell to its knees, I turned on the other three and sidestepped to get them in a line. When I came in throwing punches, they barely saw it coming. The fifth was a kick to one of their shins, and the robot's leg flew out from underneath it. My punch hit the back of its head, slamming it into the ground so hard that the metal dented.

A moment later, it was reforming, but the other robots had backed off, smooth, metallic faces staring at me. If they were humans, that would have been awe or shock.

"Not bad," Sacrada said, and I spun to see her standing in the doorway.

She walked in, looking me up and down, then said, "What tier are you?"

"I'm not a... tier."

Her brow furrowed in confusion. "You're not from here then. It's true, you're really...a descendant of Apollo?"

"Hell if I know," I admitted. "But I'm here, my powers are apparently working, so yeah, let's say I am."

She glanced away, then at the robots, who had formed a line, ready for more training if we so desired.

"What're you doing here?" I asked.

"Same as you," she replied. "Wanted something to punch. Maybe it should be you?"

I gulped. As far as I knew, and from what I'd seen back there, this lady could be the most powerful super ever. "You said something about tiers?"

"I'm sure Navani mentioned something to you about it, no?" She started moving about me, assessing me, preparing for the attack I wasn't sure I could handle. I'd had buddies in the Marines who always laughed at the idea of getting beat by a girl. Those same buddies, when put to the test, often were. And this wasn't just any lady, this was a super. One with the DNA of someone who'd been considered practically a goddess. "Very well. Tiers— basically how supers are ranked. Those like Lamb are able to analyze one's powers, see what they're capable of, and pretty much rank us."

"That sounds… horrible."

"It's not used as a way of putting anyone down," she said. "At least, it wasn't under the rule of the

Elders and the Citadel. But if Ranger comes into power? You can bet your ass that would change."

"So we can't let him."

She eyed me for a long moment, then shook her head with a look of confusion. "You actually do care, don't you? This world that isn't even yours, this galaxy, and you're ready to put your life on the line? Please tell me it's not just for the chance at some pussy."

"I'm too insulted by that to know how to answer, other than to say it's not." She was already starting to square up against me, stretching her shoulders and neck, eyeing me to gauge my reach and whatnot, so I prepared, ready to react and defend myself. "On my world, when someone's being bullied, you step up and punch the bully in the face. That doesn't stop them? Take it to the next level."

"That so?" she asked. "All Earthers are like this?"

"Ah… no."

"Just you, Mr. Chivalry?"

"Again, no. The men and women who fought at my side in the Marines, though. Any one of them would give their life to save me, and I'd do the same for them. Likewise, we see someone getting pushed around, we push back. We see someone pulling a gun on a child, we take that gun and shove it right up that son of a bitch's ass."

She grimaced.

"Figuratively," I corrected myself. "Just... to be clear."

"I'm glad to hear it. So..." She threw out a fast side kick, which I barely dodged, knocking aside. "If I were to bully you right now, what would you shove up—er, ignore that."

She moved out of the way of my counter-attack, grinning. Was she suddenly toying with me? Maybe even flirting? Or maybe it was a test.

"You're no bully," I said, refusing to take the bait. "Just a woman who cares deeply for her sister and will do whatever it takes to get her back."

The smile vanished from her face, a distant coldness there instead. "When we find him, I swear to all that is holy..." Her offensive posture was gone, replaced by a vulnerable, scared woman. "She went missing once, after graduating from the academy. We were on a vacation to celebrate, off on Yurelsa to partake in their bliss lakes—I forget, you're not from here—lakes that are like hot springs, only the steam kind of gives you a high. All the kids were into it. And there I am after, stumbling back to our room, laughing, and I turn to see I'm alone. When I finally found her, she was dead. Gone. See, she'd gotten so high she'd fallen asleep in the waters, sunk down, and nobody had noticed. The drugs worked differently on her, they said, after a super had used his powers to revive her. Lucky for us, he was there. Only one on the whole planet and, we found out later, only one anywhere close to being nearby. She would've been lost if not for him."

"That's... crazy."

She looked up at me as if remembering I was there. "What's crazy is that I was so out of it, I had somehow just left her like that. It wouldn't have even been an issue, if not for my dumb decision-making and the fact that I allowed my senses to be dulled. Never again, I told myself. And she's always looked at me differently since then, too. Like she blames herself, but also isn't sure how trusting to be around me. At the same time, if I'm not around when she tries to call, or home when she expects it, she kind of freaks out. Hell, she freaks out when I don't have her favorite rum bundt cake for her birthday, or when I put the toilet paper on the wrong way. What's she going through right now, without me there?"

I had nothing to say. The fact that she was even opening up to me like this at all was amazing, and I didn't want to ruin it by saying something stupid.

All that feeling vanished when she added, "And here I am, stuck with you sex-crazed lunatics as my best chance of saving her."

Without another word, she came at me. At least

she didn't flare her golden powers or anything like that, she was fighting straight normal-person style. Still, she was fast. When she tested me with a jab, I barely moved out of the way, her hand stopping an inch from my nose. I attempted a counterstrike, but she sidestepped and caught me in the ribs with a roundhouse kick. It was strong, pain shooting up my ribs, and yet I could tell she was holding back.

"We're going to rescue her," I said, recovering.

"Shut up."

"I'm just saying—"

BAM! Her kick took out my leg, and I flew up, then slammed down onto my back.

"Trying not to think about it until it's time to get in there and save her," she said, offering me a hand to get back up. "So how about you focus on something else. Anything else."

Taking a step back, I caught my breath and put up my fists, trying to relax. "It's not fair, you know."

"What's that?" She took a defensive stance this time, moving around me. "I'm not even using my powers."

"Sure you are. Your strongest one, from what I can tell."

"You're wrong."

I grinned, circling with her now, squared off, ready for the attack I knew would come. "Come on, with your looks? Any man would have a hard time focusing. And the last thing I'd want to do is mar that beauty."

"What the fuck?" She lowered her guard, about to laugh at my cheesiness, when I dove in, throwing a good combination of a fake jab, then a right cross, left uppercut, and another right cross. She dodged the first three, but my last hit caught her, right in the tit.

"Oh my God, I'm sorry," I said, putting my hand to my mouth.

She growled and came at me, sweeping me down and landing with her knee between my legs—not hard enough to cause damage, but enough pressure to let me know she could.

"Hit me in the breasts again, and find out if balls pop like grapes," she said.

I grabbed her by the collar, smiling. "I'm liking the foreplay."

She slapped me, using the moment to break my grip and push herself off of me.

Of course, now that I understood my powers a bit better, I'd been able to use the situation to my advantage. Had I really been hitting on her? No. Not exactly. I'd wanted her close, for a situation just like that to get my endorphins or hormones or whatever working. Maybe it was cheating, but hey, there was no way she was that fast and strong without some sort of help from her powers.

When I stood, the hype was there, working its way through me. I stretched, grinning at her, as she arched an eyebrow in curiosity.

"Something up, big guy?" she asked, glancing at my crotch to check.

"It isn't that," I said, and came at her with a flurry of strikes. She started to smile as she blocked some, took a couple more, and threw her own. "This is more like it!"

"What's that you say, you like it?" I grinned, knowing that wasn't what she'd said. "You'll love this, then."

This time I swept around behind her, grabbed her by her midsection, and tossed her over me in a move I'd learned in high school wrestling. Going with her, I landed on her back and took the proper position—forgetting, of course, that usually, that was with men. My right hand was firmly cupping her breast, though not on purpose.

She shoved me off, and we both leaped to our feet, turning to face each other. Just when I thought she was going to punch me, she pinned me up against the wall and held me there, golden eyes staring into mine.

"So what? I'm supposed to stick your dick in

me?" she asked. "I'm supposed to let some stranger cum in me to save the universe? That's fucking stupid."

"I…" I thought about what to say to that and nodded. "All I'm doing is going along for the ride. Am I drinking the kool-aid? Yes. Would I… cum… in you?" I took a deep breath. "Only if you wanted it."

Her earlier statement to Navani had made it sound like she might be more into women than men, but the look in her eyes said otherwise. I'd had my share of women in my day—I knew that look.

For another moment she held me there, seeming as if she was either about to take me right there or slam my head into the wall and storm off. Finally, she pulled me to her and kissed me. It wasn't just a simple lip press, either. Her kiss was passionate, tongue playing with mine, breathing hot and heavy, and then she was pulling back, eyes like fire, and she licked her lips with a glare.

"Right. You can fight, kinda. You'll get there. Passion?" She wiped the side of her lips. "Definitely. And your cock works, as we've all seen."

"Ah, yes. Check to all of the above."

"Good." She let me go and turned, heading for the door.

"That's it?" I asked.

"You expected me to fuck you right here, right

now?" She laughed. "No way, baby. You gotta earn my angelic pussy."

As she exited, I stared after her, watching the way that outfit hugged her ass. Everything about her was, as she'd described her pussy, angelic. That ass was the type I could take one look at and instantly be able to imagine slapping against my hips as I took her from behind, or feel in my hands as I squeezed, her riding me.

The room was back to just me and the robots, and Lamb's voice returned. "It's going well, no?"

"I'm having mixed feelings on that," I said, one finger going to my lips subconsciously, remembering the feel of Sacrada's lips pressed to mine. "But yeah, I think so."

"More sparring?"

I glanced at the robots, adjusted my boner while imagining one of them kicking me in the dick, and said, "No. Definitely not right now."

She appeared then, grinning at the way I was adjusting myself.

"You're a horny A.I., aren't you?" I asked.

Her laugh had a tinge of sorrow to it. "Again, not an A.I. And… yes. I miss it, honestly, the feeling of having a real body, the feeling of a man's body pressed against mine, entering me." For a moment she closed her eyes, took a deep breath, and then her eyes opened wide. "I'm sorry."

"No, it's perfectly fine." In fact, her deep breath and little talk made my boner grow back to pre-sex-with-Navani levels.

"Not sorry for that," she corrected, the smile that formed looking mischievous. "Sorry for what I'm about to say."

"I'm getting worried. What is it?"

She blew out, building up her courage, apparently, and then said, "Can I touch it?"

"I'm sorry, what?"

"Your cock. I mean, I know I can't actually, but I can pretend, and use the suit. You'll love it, I promise."

"I literally just came like… what was that? Thirty minutes ago? An hour at most?"

"We don't have to finish," she said, appearing in front of me, her translucent hand hovering over the bulge in my pants but waiting, a look of begging in her eyes.

I nodded, and when her hand pressed against me, the suit reacted. I knew she wasn't actually touching me, and that she could make the suit do this without her appearing right there, but it probably worked better for her this way.

And suddenly the suit was moving all over me,

and it was bliss, unlike anything I'd ever felt. Imagine if you had hands on your balls, your ass, your legs, massaging your back, caressing your abs and chest—all of this at once.

I reached down, eagerly pulling out my cock, and reached to grab her by the head. I wanted to feel her mouth around me, or maybe take her and rip her clothes off and fuck her like nobody had ever been fucked before. My body was still feeling the rejuvenated powers from my interaction with Sacrada, I realized, and thought about the implications this power could have for my sex life.

My hand went through thin air, the sensation around my dick was gone, and Lamb pulled back, frowning. The sensation around the rest of me died off, all but the feeling of her hand on my balls, caressing them, playing with them.

"Dear, sexy man…" She shook her head, eyes sad. "You know I'm not really here. You can't touch me, and when it's out," she glanced down at my cock, "as tasty as that thick sausage looks, I can't do a damn thing with it."

And then she was gone.

"Lamb…" I started, but what could I say. She knew I hadn't been thinking, that I was an idiot. I had been so caught up in the moment. In a sense, it was like she had a handicap and I'd been incredibly insensitive about it. Her handicap was a strange one —she didn't have a body, and was essentially dead, or dying.

A strange situation, for sure.

"Oh, there you are," Navani said, entering. She froze, seeing me there with my dick out, and just stared, mouth open.

"I can explain," I said.

She closed her mouth, and I thought she was going to yell at me, but instead, she just started laughing. She laughed, tried to stop, and then laughed some more.

"I don't know if anyone's ever told you," I said, putting my cock away. "Guys don't really like it when you laugh at seeing their dicks."

"And I don't know if I told you," she said, holding back her laughter for a moment, "but usually we spar in *our* galaxy with our genitals concealed. But hey, whatever gets you off." And then the laughing returned. She let it die down, chuckling and wiping her eyes, then motioned for me to follow her. "Come on, weirdo. We're about to jump, and I thought you'd like to see this."

10

On the ship's bridge, Sacrada was strapped into one of the seats and glanced up at me, nodding with a look of interest. Navani looked at me with curiosity, then Sacrada, and her smile widened.

"I miss something here?" she asked.

"No," Lamb's voice came in as she appeared, walking past us. *Not suspicious at all*, I thought sarcastically. The other two didn't seem to notice, however, as they were busy staring at each other— Sacrada with a glare, Navani with her knowing smile.

Lamb stopped at the display. "Approaching jump gate."

Whatever we'd all been thinking, it didn't matter

when the gate came into view. I got the impression that Sacrada had never seen this type of gate either, because she was leaning forward, those beautiful golden eyes wide with excitement.

Ahead of us, forming between stars in space, was a bright, purple light. It was like someone had traced the lines to connect the images of several stars, and then cast some magic on it. I knew better. This was the result of one of their supers and his powers. The Elder they called Hadrian.

I couldn't imagine what would be possible with the power to create gateways in the stars. If I could create a portal to anywhere in the universe, what would I be capable of? Thinking it through, however, I started to realize it might not be the best idea. Who knows if I might create a gate to a black hole or a random spot in space and suddenly die? Maybe end up on a planet of robot dinosaurs or mind-reading people who were half-robot spiders. That got me thinking, wondering if maybe this guy could only create gateways to places he'd been before.

Those thoughts all left my mind as we drew closer and the dazzling light enchanted me. I'd never seen anything like it.

"Try not to shit your pants," Lamb said with a

wink. The comment earned a roll of Sacrada's eyes, though Navani laughed.

"Just get us there, and we'll all promise to use the potty, mommy," Navani countered.

"There's a good girl." Lamb grinned as the ship accelerated.

Moments later we were passing through the purple light, everything around us warping. Sound stopped, my head felt like it was being pulled in two directions at once. Then, in a blink of an eye, we were through. Just like that, we had shot through space.

And... it looked exactly the same.

"Did we... do it?

"Not a question men like to be asked," Lamb said. "But yes, we're in and already out."

"Lamb!" Navani chided her, while Sacrada frowned. "We have company."

"My apologies," Lamb replied, giving me a wink.

"My sister was the demon to my angel," Sacrada said. "I never liked the way she spoke, but hearing it from you certainly isn't a shock."

I gave her a sideways glance. Her type was likely to be the dirtiest once the doors were closed, and I'd already seen a different side of her, somewhat, in the dojo. My mind was racing with different versions of what she might really be like under the sheets.

The ship changed course, and I saw a planet ahead, an asteroid belt past it and bright stars beyond. No sign of the enemy yet, though.

"Where are they?" I asked.

"They've seen that, even when surrounded, we can outmaneuver them," Navani explained. "My bet? They're sticking true to their word, and Goros will be with his army at the ruins outside of Demekal."

"Couldn't we just nuke 'em then?"

Lamb laughed. "I've heard of you Earthers and the legendary nukes. Got a spider? Nuke it. Some country causing your problems? Nuke it. Burrito?"

"Nuke it," I said, wishing she hadn't said burrito and filled my mind with images of guacamole seeping out of a greasy tortilla. "Still didn't answer me, but I'll take your mockery as a 'no.'"

"You can imagine that superpowers have given our scientists the ability to create much stronger weapons than nukes."

"Damn."

"Yeah," Lamb turned to me with a proud smile, as if she'd been largely responsible for developing such weapons. For all I knew, she had. "Thing is, we aren't equipped with anything *that* powerful, and if we were it would cause so many casualties—probably including taking out ourselves—that it wouldn't be worth it."

"And if we had nukes," Navani chimed in, "they likely have detection systems in place, good defenses, and a fallback plan."

"Meaning?"

"Goros will have his strongest warriors on the ground to take us down, but he probably left some ships off-planet, ready to move in and strike or get him out of there if there's a problem. It's what I would do, with a fleet like his."

I nodded, getting it.

"But we have other issues to discuss, in the meantime," Navani said, turning her chair to better see Sacrada.

"The prophecy again?" Sacrada said, glancing at me warily as if I were the one to come up with it. Come to think about it, what a genius move that would've been! Go back in time and tell a bunch of hotties that they would have to fuck me to create the savior so that they'd pick me up in their spaceship and ride me till I died of exhaustion.

"Not a prophecy," Navani replied, exasperated. "Listen. It's simple science. His parents carried the most powerful genes, genes that, according to our scientists, if mixed with the genes of our incredible mother, would do wonders. Create the strongest super to ever breathe air in this galaxy."

"But there's no guarantee he'd be a hero. He could just as easily go villain."

"Not with our guidance!" Navani was seething. "You think I'd allow my child to go corrupt?"

"Your child now?"

"I—well…"

Sacrada leaned in, fingers steepled under her chin. "So, what, you plan on raising this child no matter whose it is? You'd take my baby from me?"

"What, no! Or, yes." Navani turned to Lamb for help, but she was wisely focusing on flying in a way that seemed more likely to be purposefully avoiding this conversation. With a sigh, Navani continued. "I've accepted it as my duty, should any of you be unable. I know you have your own lives and that this is a great burden."

"But seven months wouldn't be?"

"Ah, you mean nine?" I asked.

Lamb chuckled. "Silly Earther. Not here, not for supers—even the most mundane of us up here have accelerated development and nourishment, leading to pregnancies that only last seven months… as rare as pregnancies are."

"You have to have some, or you wouldn't have this sort of population," I pointed out.

"Ah, of course. But don't forget, long lives."

"And most supers fuck like," Sacrada turned to

me, "as you say on Earth, fuck like bunnies. Even with the low chance of pregnancy, you take into account the fact that supers are going at it like five times a day when married, you can see how there would still be babies born from time to time."

"Right," Lamb agreed. "Chance of pregnancy is extremely low, that doesn't mean actual pregnancies are so rare."

"Well, interesting. Wait a sec, five times a day?" I tried to process that. At most, I think I'd done three times in a day, maybe four.

"After being married for a while, that's right," Navani said. "Before that, hell, I did ten in a day once. Granted, that's when I had my troupe of supers, and we'd—"

"Whoa, whoa." I held up my hands. "That's not an image I want in my head. Not if we're going to be... you know."

"Ah, isn't that cute," Sacrada said, mocking me. "He thinks you're like his girlfriend or something."

"What? I didn't say that."

Navani gave me a curious glance, then turned back to Lamb. "How're we looking?"

"Coming in fast," Lamb said, rolling easily with the change in subject.

"Right." Navani glanced back at us, pausing long enough that any of us could've brought the conversation back to where it had been. We let it slide, to my relief. "In that case, we should discuss strategy for once we arrive."

"Charge in there and get my sister back," Sacrada replied. "Where's the debate?"

Navani nodded but held up a finger. "We'll need help. If we had one more sister…"

"You'd leave Sakurai with this madman one second longer than necessary?"

"But if we might lose without Threed, then it might be necessary," Navani countered.

"Threed?" Sacrada asked, and the look of horror in her eyes showed that wasn't a good thing. "Oh, hell no. You can go fuck yourself."

"And here I thought your sister was the crude one," I said. "That mouth…"

"Fuck you, too!" she said, turning on me now. "Do you have any idea who this is they want to go after?"

I shook my head. "Another sister, no?"

"Yes, but the craziest of the bunch. Last time I saw her, she was on some *discover her lineage* trip and I tried to help her. Woke up one day with her trying to set me on fire! She said she was curious about my powers, wondered what would happen."

"Wouldn't you be okay?" I asked.

"That's beside the point! And… no. Not if I was

asleep and didn't have time to process it and I ignited. I'm not immune to flames in my normal state."

"Damn."

"Damn is right!" She stood now, pacing along the bridge. "I was staying with a man at the time, this really big guy, and the gentleman type, or so I thought."

"She tried to seduce him?" I asked.

"No! I woke up with him in bed and he was still asleep, but she was there, slowly undoing his pants, carefully so as not to wake him. I was groggy, didn't understand what was happening, and then she takes out his dick and puts it in her mouth!"

"What the fuck?" Navani was, it seemed, starting to understand that Threed wasn't normal, though she sounded kinda fun to me. Not the fire part, of course. "What'd you do?"

"I watched until she made my man cum," Sacrada said, deadpan.

"Really?" Lamb asked, also getting into it.

"NO!" Sacrada's eyes lit up, her skin starting to glow too. "I kicked her in her fucking face. Of course, I forgot that she still had my man's dick in her mouth. The pain caused her to bite down—not hard enough to do any lasting damage, but... he left me after that. After hiding in the corner like a timid little pussycat while Threed and I went at each other. Meaning, I beat the shit out of her. When she left, she acted like *I* was the one who'd done something wrong! Said there was no way we could be sisters, even from a different dad, and said she would never leave home again. Then told me my man's dick tasted like peppermint and asked him if she could kiss it all better for him. The fucking nerve!"

"Dammmmnnn," I said, leaning back and trying my best not to imagine a woman biting down. Mood killer, for sure.

The other two stood there in silence for a long moment, until finally, Navani said, "The fact remains, she's one of the sisters. We can't rule her out of the mission, and she might be key to rescuing Sakurai."

Sacrada stared at her, eyebrows raised, and then turned and stormed out of there.

"She didn't finish the story," Lamb said. "Did she say yes or no, about kissing it better?"

"No," I said. "Just a hunch."

"Where's she going?" Navani asked. "Dammit. Dammit!"

"I'll go after her I said," standing to pursue.

"You want me to come?" Navani asked, then blushed at the look I gave her. "I guess I can't call you a pervert, considering the circumstances. But I meant—"

"No, stay here. I got it."

The hallway outside of the door was already empty, so I imagine Sacrada had taken off running. That meant she had energy she wanted to burn off. The dojo. I charged down the passages to it, then paused to catch my breath before moving to the sliding doors.

A blast of hot air hit me as they opened, and I stumbled back, throwing up my hands. Within, I saw Sacrada going at it, moving in what almost looked like a dance as she took down robots left and right. Her tight outfit clung to her, showing off taut muscles and her perfect ass, breasts bouncing slightly with each attack—as much as the outfit would allow. Her wings spread out, sunbursts blasting robots into their molten forms.

She continued like this for another minute, until there were none left. The metal started to reform but was too hot to do so.

Her eyes met mine, and the fire died off. "You…"

"I'm sorry. About your man." I stepped toward the room, but it was still too hot, and I had to move back to the hall.

"He wasn't good for me anyway," she said.

"Not a good man?"

She laughed. "No, it isn't that... it was..."

"Yeah?"

"Well, his, you know... it was just too big. Hurt like hell. And I mean every damn time. I kept thinking I'd learn to like it, that it would feel good eventually, but really it just hurt."

"I don't know if I want to hear this."

"Because you think I'm one of your girlfriends, right?" she said, an eyebrow arching. "You're going to get jealous if your girlfriend talks about some man she used to fuck?" Walking over to me, she kept on. "Let's see if I got this right because I'm still trying to process it. Me, who every super alive would love to date, should give it up to you like that because my half-sister says so. And when I talk about some other man's penis, that's right, I said penis, you get all squirmy because in that twisted mind of yours, you've allowed that woman to convince you that I'm yours?"

"No," I said, hating that there might be some truth to all that. "I came back here to see if you need to talk, if I can comfort you somehow."

"Is that right?" She folded her arms. "Sure, take it out and let's fuck. That'll make me feel better, and we can accomplish our steps toward the prophecy, too."

"Um, really?"

"NO!" she stood a couple of paces away from me, staring me down, then scoffed. "Damn, you'd really do it too, wouldn't you? If I'd been serious, you would've done it. Just pulled it out right here and done me in the hallway. Nothing about that seems wrong to you?"

"I..."

Whatever I'd been about to say was ruined by the fact that, for some reason, everything she was saying was causing me to get hard. As my boner started to show, she glanced down and snorted in derision.

"Point proven," she said and started to walk off through the hallway that led up to the viewing deck. I hated myself for checking out her ass as she walked, but you don't get a view like that every day. Plus, I quickly looked away.

Was she right about me? I had to hope not... but maybe all of this mumbo-jumbo Navani kept throwing my way was changing me? When a man thinks about sex all of the time, it's hard to change tracks mid-run.

"Sacrada," I called after her.

She spun on me, hands on her hips. "What?"

"We're going to rescue her. Whatever I can do to ensure that happens, I promise I'll do. Okay?"

"Okay." She waited to see if there was anything more to add.

"And… sex or no sex, prophecy be damned, I'm here for you."

She blinked, considering me, and then said, "Thanks."

Then she turned around and walked off. She needed some alone time, I got that. If this had been some crazy porno, I imagined the guy would've gone up there after her, only to find her completely naked. She'd tear off his clothes and jump his bones finally, the stars around them as they went at each other like the animals they were.

Only, this wasn't one of those movies. I was a gentleman, and she needed her space.

I turned back down the hall and jumped with surprise. Navani stood there at the corner, leaning against the wall, watching me.

"That was… sweet," she said.

"It's true. I'm not here just to have sex with you all, even if that's how you see me. I'm more than just cock and balls."

"You're right. You're a nice guy, sorta." She grinned. "But that part of you is nice too."

"Says the woman who walked away without saying anything after we…"

"Fucked?" She nodded. "That's all it was. What do you expect?"

"Maybe… and I hate myself for saying this, but maybe… maybe that's not enough."

"Don't be a little girl about this."

I frowned. "There's so much wrong with what you just said. Regardless of what this makes me, I like emotions to be involved. Have I had meaningless sex? Of course. Women love a man in uniform. But being used, then discarded like I'm nobody? Some guys might kill for that opportunity, but I'm not one of them. Especially if you consider the fact that, at least while this is going on, you're my only friends."

"We're friends now?"

"I don't fucking know what we are," I shouted, not wanting to raise my voice but not stopping it either. "That's my point! When this is over, what, I just go home? There's nothing there for me anyway. My buddies… half have died in the wars, the others are still out there serving in a military I'm done with. My brother was the only one I really wanted to see, and I understand he's out here in this galaxy of crazy supers too. So what happens after all this?"

"Whatever you want to happen." She considered me for a moment, then walked over. Stopping in front of me, she took my hand in hers, considered it, then lifted it to her mouth and kissed it.

"I'm… I'm not sure what that means," I admitted. "On Earth, a guy kisses a woman's hand."

"Here it means a woman likes a guy. She chooses him, in a sense. She lets him into her…"

"Heart?"

"I don't want to say that, but yes, usually?" She kissed my hand again, a strange curiosity in her eyes. "It was awkward before not because I had *no* feelings, but exactly because I'm starting to feel something. That scares me. It's not supposed to happen."

I took her hand to my lips this time, pressing them gently against her soft skin. She giggled but didn't pull away.

"It's silly," she said. "We barely know each other."

"And there's the fact that you're trying to get me to sleep with your sisters."

"Yes, and that." She shrugged. "But, you know, as much as you seem to feel awkward when one of us talks about an ex or something related, I don't think it's the same here."

"How so?" I asked.

"I just mean, this is what we have to do. This whole situation, and I don't know. I don't think seeing you with another woman would make me feel like any less of a woman, or that your feelings toward me would be any less. If anything, that might be a good thing, since we don't know where your future lies."

I scrunched my nose. "Or if I'll even live through this fight with Goros."

"Any of us," she agreed. "So yeah, we have to make the best of our situation. Do whatever we can to see that our mission is fulfilled."

"The prophecy."

"Don't call it that." She looked into my eyes, then grinned.

"What?"

"Want to test it?" she asked. "We still have time before we land."

"I'm not following."

Her smile widened. "Trust me." Next, she spoke to the ship as she said, "Lamb, can you join us in the jungle room?"

"Gladly," Lamb's voice replied.

Without any more explanation, Navani took me by the hand and led me along another passage, turned, and led me to a wide set of doors. They opened, and we entered. Inside it was steamy, the sound of a waterfall nearby, trees and vines surrounding a soft floor similar to the mats in the dojo.

"What's this?" I asked.

Lamb appeared on the floor, not in the same outfit she'd worn on the deck, but in a robe that left one shoulder and her cleavage exposed, reminding me of Ancient Greece.

"A room set up to ease the tension," Lamb explained, then turned to Navani. "How can I help here? I thought we were reserving this room for... later."

"I want to test my emotions," Navani said.

"And that involves me?"

"Yes. I want you to simulate a threesome with him." Navani glanced my way, a sparkle in her eye. "The three of us."

My boner had definitely returned, and when Lamb stepped up to me, moving her hands across me and my suit responding in kind, I barely processed the fact that she wasn't really doing this, that her hands weren't really touching me. Then hands were reaching around, pulling out my cock, and stroking it, and I looked down to see they were Navani's hands. Her lips found mine, and for a moment we kissed, but then she pulled back to watch Lamb as the woman knelt and mimicked giving me head. Navani stroked, Lamb moved her head in the motion while sending pleasure sensors through my suit. It was the ultimate handjob, while the sensors made it feel like Lamb had her hands on my balls, rubbing along my ass, caressing my inner thighs and back.

"No issues?" I asked between heavy breaths, watching Navani.

"I like it," she said, and then lowered herself to join Lamb. There was really only one woman there, but it felt like five. Finally, Navani tore off her clothes, then mine, and started riding me. The jungle fog rose up behind her, and I watched as her breasts bounced with each motion, her eyes staring back at mine. Lamb started to leave, but Navani held out a hand and said, "Wait. Watch… if you want."

She helped me stand, and the three of us made it over to the small waterfall. When she guided me to it, I resisted, but her smile was reassuring, her eyes comforting. To my surprise, the water was warm. We waded in, and she started washing me—every inch, while Lamb watched. I returned the favor, and then we reclined on a bank of simulated moss, where she straddled me and slid herself onto my cock.

Lamb smiled, reached up and undid the clasp on her robe, then let it fall. In the fog, I could almost believe she was really there, in the flesh. And damn, that flesh looked good. Her cute little nipples stuck out, one of her hands caressing them as her other traced her abs and then found her clit. She touched herself while watching us, moaning and licking her lips.

Meanwhile, Navani was still riding me, eyes glancing back and forth, enjoying it all as much as I was.

For a moment, Lamb smirked, and her image flashed—changing into that of Sacrada. The sight of her suddenly there and touching herself like that was nearly enough to make me cum, but I turned away and said, "No, not until it's real." She smiled and turned back to herself. My reaction made Navani ride me even harder, and within seconds she was moaning and yelping, and then she let out a long moan of pleasure. I felt extra damp down there, but she didn't stop, only rolled me over so I could take charge.

I grabbed her legs and pulled them over my shoulders, squeezing her thighs firmly, and plunged back into her. Lamb appeared in front of me as if kneeling over Navani's face, as she continued to touch her breasts, moving them in front of my face. There was the image of her like that, and Navani's perfect body beneath me. Combined with the pleasure of feeling Navani's warm skin and moist pussy, I closed my eyes and opened my mouth, feeling the surge in my cock as it grew to its limit, and then shot into Navani.

She moaned, loving it, and reached down

between us to rub my balls as I came again and again until I was finally spent.

When we were done, Lamb lay down with us, staring up at the simulated blue sky.

"That was... amazing," I said.

"Perfect," Navani added.

"I'm sorry," Lamb said, propping herself up. Her breasts fell, and I wanted to lean over and kiss them, pouting at the fact that I couldn't.

"Sorry for what?" I asked.

"That I'm not able to really be there with you two. I can tell it would be great, and that you would both take care of me."

"You've sacrificed a great deal for us," Navani told her. "Never apologize for anything ever again. And thank you, for what you've just done."

"It helped?"

"And now jealousy?" I asked.

Navani just lay back, closed her eyes, and said, "Again, it was amazing. If anything, it all turned me on. I'm not exactly into women... but the idea of it all, the flesh, the pleasing of *my man*," she grinned at me with those words, "it couldn't get better than that. Well, maybe with another woman or two."

"Do you think Sacrada will come around?" Lamb asked.

Navani shrugged. "Something tells me she'll feel differently once we've rescued her sister."

"If," Lamb corrected her. "The chances of our success aren't great. I calculated them and—"

"Lamb," Navani interrupted.

"Yes?"

"Shut up and enjoy the moment. And don't forget, there's always Threed."

A feeling of unease came over me. "Are we sure about her? After everything Sacrada said…"

"My research on her shows she's not all bad," Lamb said.

"You didn't listen to the stories?" I asked.

Lamb simply smiled. "Sure, but there are always rumors that are true, and those that aren't. Maybe all of that happened, who knows. But there was one story I came across that I certainly hope falls on the side of truth."

"Don't tell us some stupid story about her saving a cat from a burning garbage pile," Navani said, closing her eyes and lying back.

"Not exactly," Lamb said with a confused laugh. "And maybe you won't be as impressed as I was, but it at least points to her humanity. Less than a year ago, she was on the front lines of the battle of Porolay, working to establish a colony out on the fringe."

"Bullshit," Navani said, opening her eyes again.

"That's what the reports say. Sure, they have notes about how she mouthed off, had multiple cases of fraternization and indecent exposure, but when it came down to it, and a group of soldiers were out there, cut off and told no help was coming, she said fuck that and went off on her own. Took a mech and as many weapons as she could find and rode off on her own. Was nearly killed, but dammit, she saved every last one of those supers. They did their part of course, but every single one of them said they owed their lives to her."

"And how come I've never heard of this?" Navani asked.

"When they tried to promote her and give her a medal, she walked, threatening them, saying they had better not make it public. They never did, though it's accessible to supers like myself."

Navani shook her head, eyes distant in thought as she processed this.

"Still," I said, thinking that sounded wonderful if my life was on the line, but otherwise I wasn't sold. "Are we totally, one-hundred percent sure?"

Lamb rolled her eyes and turned away, annoyed.

"The story was great," I said in my defense. "It's just, that doesn't make her any less batshit crazy. If anything—"

"And if Threed is the most fertile of us all?" Navani cut me off. "We can't throw away that chance based on a feud."

"I'm more worried about her burning down the ship," I admitted. "Or, you know, her biting off my dick."

"We won't let that happen," Navani said, leaning over to me and caressing my now half-limp cock. "Not to my precious."

For some reason, that word choice gave me an odd feeling, but I couldn't remember why, so pushed the thought from my mind.

"She's right," Lamb said. "About Threed and needing to try other wombs. Also, the woman will be incredibly useful in the fight against Goros."

I nodded, knowing it wasn't my place to argue. Hell, it wasn't the first time I'd fucked a crazy chick, at least. Although, in the past, I'd always found out *after* the fact. When Lamb told us it was time to get dressed and head to the bridge, and that Sacrada was already there, waiting, we got to it and I pushed my worry aside.

Whatever happened, I'd make it happen and do my best. I just had to remember to be careful, and play it right with Sacrada. From where I stood, I'd gladly fuck her any day of the week over some crazy, dick-biting pyromaniac.

11

A rolla had a pleasant pink hue to the planet, explained to me as being a result of the distance of the planet's sun and the makeup of its ozone layer. We approached Demekal, noting hills in the distance and vast jungles elsewhere.

"The ruins," Lamb said, indicating the hills.

"In the hills?" I asked.

"The ruins *are* the hills."

For some reason, I'd imagined we would be fighting Goros in a much smaller area than this. Now I understood the odd shapes of the hills, the way they looked like walls from a distance.

"Please tell me there aren't giant jungle snakes or

spiders out there," I said. "Tell me that, and I'll be fine. No worries."

Sacrada was the one to laugh now. "Is he serious?" She turned to me. "Honey, the ruins of Melatand are famed for their beasts—spiders being chief among them. But I didn't know you had spiders back home. Interesting."

"Yeah, lots of spiders…" A shiver ran up my spine at the thought.

"Well, only one giant snake around here we have to worry about," Lamb said with a smile my way.

"Lamb!" Navani said with an apologetic glance Sacrada's way.

"Oh, get over it," Lamb said. "Everyone keeps assuming that because I worked with the Elders and that because I'm kinda dead, I shouldn't have a healthy sexual appetite."

Did that make me a bit of a necro-whatever they call people who have sex with the dead? It wasn't like that, right? I mean, she was more like an A.I., like a virtual reality simulation on crack. I shook my head, trying not to focus on little things like that.

Oddly, her joke had made me forget about the spiders. Even letting my mind wander back to them, I felt less worried. Something about a woman like her complimenting my dick just made all the worries seem less important. I laughed at myself at the thought that life and death situations might be somehow diminished in importance simply because my ego had been fed. How many other guys would be so shallow? At least I acknowledged it.

"So, Threed…" Navani said, turning to meet Sacrada's gaze. "We need to go after her. We have to get her on board."

"Why not any of the others first?" Sacrada asked. "The one they call the Blue Lady now, for instance. Why couldn't we just go get her, then come back for the fight?"

"Alesa, AKA Tunnel, now AKA the Blue Lady." Lamb scrunched her nose. "Last known position, incarcerated."

"Meaning," Navani explained, "that we'd have to break into the prison ship and rescue her. Thing is, that's impossible."

"Actually," Lamb had images flickering across the screen. "Not for long."

"What?"

Lamb turned to me and smiled as one of the images froze. I couldn't believe it—my brother was there with two hot chicks, one with green hair and the other wearing some sort of silly fox ears and heavy mascara. They appeared to be running…

"I don't understand," I said.

"Your brother, his mission is in effect."

"He's going to save the Blue Lady?"

"Uh, technically he doesn't know she's involved." Lamb glanced around, grimacing. "She wasn't added to the list because of her... newly villainous ways."

"So there's my answer," Sacrada said, seemingly done with the topic.

I wasn't, however. "My brother? *My* little bro?" I laughed. "No way, that's a fake. He's no hero."

"Zero to hero," Navani said, nodding. "Classic hero story."

"No, but I mean all he does is work and watch old movies and make fun of Planet Kill. Get this, most popular show ever, and he says it's stupid, barbaric. Can't stand the blood and—"

"He's changed," Lamb said, freezing a new image on the screen of my brother, bodies around him. Some sort of energy seemed to be forming between his hands, black on the inside and blue on the outside, and he looked like a new man. "My point," she continued, "is that Chad, AKA Breaker, is growing very close to actually setting things right there. The Blue Lady might be back in play again soon."

"And if she's still on her quest for revenge?" Navani asked. "We can't risk that."

"Even for your *mission?*" Sacrada asked, smiling at the turn of the tide.

"Do you have any pictures of her?" Navani asked Lamb.

"Let me see," Lamb went through a few more images of my brother fighting, and my mind kept getting blown over and over. He was becoming an actual badass. Not someone to make fun of with my friends anymore, that was for sure. The little boy who would insist on wearing his underwear over his pants and pretending to fly was now becoming a superhero, just like me.

An image of him with those same two women, again, froze on the screen, all three nude, the fox-ear wearing lady with his cock in her mouth.

"Oh, damn," Navani exclaimed, and Sacrada groaned while I laughed.

"My little bro's a badass!" I said.

The others looked at me, then nodded or said they agreed. He certainly seemed to have grown one.

She quickly flicked to the next image, one of him dressed again, staring in a mixture of horror and amazement as metal seemed to have twisted and distorted around him into a tunnel, a woman, all blue, walking toward him. Or, more like floating.

"That's her?" I asked.

Navani said it was, but then sat there staring at the image for a moment. So was I, though I had to admit my thoughts were a tad more inappropriate than I imagine hers were. As scary and intimidating as this Blue Lady looked, she was damn hot. There was something about the arch of her brows, her high cheekbones, and pursed lips, that made me think she would dominate the fuck out of me in the bedroom, and maybe I'd like that.

"Would she be an excellent ally?" Navani asked. "Yes. Would we be able to get her in time to help fight Goros and save your sister, Sacrada? Not a chance. I'm sorry."

Sacrada nodded.

"She might, however," Navani turned to me now, curious, "be next on our list after this is over. If we can trust her."

"What exactly did she do to end up in this prison?" I asked.

"Murdered a few high-tier supers, some good, some bad," Lamb answered. "The claim on her part is that they were all involved, or working to support, a supervillain who destroyed her birthplace and all the people who lived there."

"So she was sent to this prison ship," I said, getting it.

"Maybe," Lamb replied. "But some think she went there to finish her revenge. That someone, or multiple someones, on that ship was her next target. Me? I doubt it was the last piece of the puzzle, however. I think she's going to be a bit of a gamble in this endeavor."

All thoughts of ramming her from behind as I pulled on that beautiful blue hair started to fade. This chick sounded batshit crazy, and maybe we didn't need that.

"The thing is," Navani interjected, "we can figure that out next. Check in when we've saved Sakurai. Until then, we have our mission, and the steps to getting it done. Lamb, pull up Threed."

Lamb did so, while I tried to push the image of my brother and those two chicks out of my mind.

On the screen now was the image of probably the craziest looking woman I'd ever seen. She stared at us with mismatched eyes of red and blue, eyes that resembled old-school 3D glasses. They didn't seem to fit, those mismatched eyes, and I stared at them for a long moment, wondering if the red eye was some sort of cyborg implant, or what. Her mouth was turned up in a wicked grin, her bright, pink hair shaved on the side and combed over to the other side. She also had pink tattoos on her shoulders and upper thighs, which were both exposed in the black and violet outfit she wore.

"Called Threed because of her ability to create replicas of herself, similar to 3D printing," Lamb explained, throwing off my guess that it was related to the old-school blue and red glasses, "Threed can make up to two copies at any given time, no more. In theory, she could, I suppose, but it would take too much focus. But it's not just her though. She's able to make replicas of those around her, of objects too. Anything up to about the size of two of herself, give or take."

"So not a building," I clarified. "Or a ship."

"That's right. Although there are supers known for their ability to amplify others, to our knowledge Threed has never gone beyond her limits."

"I see why you want her," Sacrada said, glowering. "Three of me in the battle... that would have its advantages."

"Yes," Navani replied, curtly. "Three of you, or other combinations of us."

Sacrada scoffed, apparently amused by the idea that anyone would go into a fight with anything less than three of her if given the option. "Oh, you're serious? Sorry."

"These replicas, how long do they stay in play?" I asked. "I mean, do they have a shelf life?"

"Until she wants to create a new one, or loses her focus," Lamb answered. "If she's getting the shit kicked out of her, for example, we lose whatever replicas she's created."

"So the battle plan is," Navani said, "we get her

and keep her safe enough to continue replicating us in the battle based on what powers make the most sense at any given moment."

"Okay, so if we all suddenly need a good lay, she makes two of loverboy here," Sacrada said, then looked pensive before adding, "Actually, a question there—would a replica's sperm still be able to do the job?"

I frowned, not sure how much I liked the idea of two fake mes getting to do the deed.

"Let's assume not," Navani said. "And... stay focused."

"Sure, sure, why the hell not?" Sacrada leaned back, arms folded. "Oh, I remember—because your crazy ass fucking plan has more holes than a fuck-cushion after this guy's done with it?"

"A fuck cushion?" I asked, too curious to be offended.

"I'll buy you one for your next birthday so you can see for yourself," she said with a wave of her hand as if dismissing me. As if my voice in all this didn't matter.

"You know, for someone who prides herself on being the angelic sister, you sure act like a bitch."

"What the fuck did you just call me?" She turned on me, eyes glowing gold. Maybe I didn't want to piss her off.

"Sorry, I didn't mean it like that. But seriously, you don't talk like an angel, that's for damn sure."

"I'm the angelic one," she said. "Not an actual angel. Means I don't dress like a slut or give hand jobs for money. Okay? Now if you're satisfied, how about we both agree that the next time you call me a bitch, I fry your face off and eat it like bacon?"

"Agreed," I said, trying very hard not to think that was a bitchy and disgusting thing to say. Also, the slut comment—while Sacrada didn't wear an ultra-tiny skirt like her sister, her battle suit was mighty revealing. Hell, I wasn't complaining about the fact that it was so tight you could even see the shape of her belly button, and that you didn't need much imagination to picture her nude.

But if that was her idea of being less slutty, sure. *Surrrre.*

"Now that that little spat's over with," Navani chided us, "how about we land this bitch and get on with it?"

Sacrada wore an expression that showed she wasn't sure about the use of the word so soon after I'd used it to refer to her, but she didn't say anything.

We were pulling up to the edge of the city, and my focus had left the conversation to take in this sight. Other ships were coming and going, several patrols making their rounds. The city was the opposite of the place in the short, rolling dunes where we'd picked up Sacrada. Here it was tall spires, thick slabs of metal that stood upright, and spikes sticking out from the metal.

No, not spikes I realized—turrets.

"It's a military city?" I asked.

"That's correct," Lamb said. With a movement of her hands, several of the metal slabs lit up on our display, green lines assessing them. "The spires on the outside are a combination of missiles and sensors, these buildings are mobile defense shields. Line them up, an energy shield forms around the city, or wherever they're needed. They also have anti-aircraft missiles loaded, and a small fleet."

"I see why Goros didn't want to attack the city."

"Yes, this could've helped keep him away, though I imagine Ranger could send more forces and take this place down fairly easily."

"As he did the Citadel," Sacrada added.

"Not completely fallen," Lamb argued.

"Not that."

That comment earned Sacrada glares from the other two, but I was confused. "They're on the same side as the Citadel, no? So why did they even let Goros into orbit, much less land?"

"They're officially on the same side, but now that the Citadel has fallen, I imagine we'll find many of the outer realms doubting their allegiances."

"And if they find out we're with the Citadel?"

"We're not," Sacrada said. "At least, not all of us."

"If they find out," Navani interjected, ignoring Sacrada's comment, "we'll find some friends and some enemies. It's the nature of the beast."

We were hailed by the local guard and given clearance, soon flying down into what appeared to be the base of one of those tall metal things, but was actually an opening just beneath it.

They had us exit the ship and go through scans, but when their system didn't recognize me or understand my powers, a large man guided me off to the side. I looked back to Navani and Sacrada for help, but the woman they started arguing with simply ignored them. The man led me into a metal room lined with mirrors.

"What is this, a disguise?" the man asked.

Figuring the truth would work best here, I explained, "I'm a Marine, from Earth."

"From Earth?" The man laughed. "That's a good one."

"It's the truth. I'm here to help them with a mission against Ranger."

"Uh huh." The guy was barely listening now. He

went to the door and opened it before calling out, "Check this guy's story out."

A moment later, he returned with the woman from outside. She was almost as large as him, though in a beautiful way. I was starting to wonder if, in most people out here having some sort of superpower, the same mutations had caused an attractive gene to dominate.

"Tell her where you're from," the man commanded.

"Earth," I repeated. "As I explained—"

He started cracking up, his laughter causing his belly to jiggle. The woman, however, glared at me and said, "Strip."

"What?"

"You heard me. Search."

I looked at the man for help, but he was still laughing, now holding his hands up and saying, "Not me. I'm not doing it to this whackjob."

"Strip," the woman said, ignoring the guy and pulling out a glove that she starting putting on.

"You've gotta be kidding," I said, looking around at the mirrors as if I hoped to see through and catch a glimpse of Navani coming to rescue me.

"Two choices here," the woman said, lifting her other hand to show a shock of electricity run across it. "Strip, or get shocked the fuck up. Either way, I get my jollies."

"This can't be allowed," I said to the man.

"Considering the fact that you're not showing up in our search, I'd say you better hurry and do what the fuck she says," the man finally said. "You're either some sort of terrorist or a spy, and we mean to find out which."

Another thirty seconds passed, then the woman stepped forward, electricity lighting up around her hand.

"Okay, okay," I protested pulling off my upper body armor. "But just to show I'm not concealing anything."

"You have five, four..."

As she spoke, I quickly undid the clasps of my lower body armor, stepping out of it. While it was technically the liquid metal biotech armor form Lamb, in situations like this, it acted just like any other armor.

She cleared her throat and nodded at my briefs.

"No fucking way," I said, glaring at the two of them.

She grabbed me and then I felt a shock running through my body that hurt, although it was more of a surprise than anything. She reached, knelt, and pulled off my undies, and in the same motion, she had the gloved hand on my ass, two fingers doing their search.

I yelped and shouted, "Get the fuck off, er, out of me!"

And she pulled them out with a pop. Without a glance at the glove, she pulled it off and tossed it in a trash receptacle that jutted out from the wall and then vanished again. A glance at the mirrors and I froze, feeling very awkward at being totally naked like that, and seeing my own ass and front at the same time.

"Can I dress now?"

"How're you hiding your identity?" she asked, eyes roaming across my nude form in a way that I knew couldn't be allowed. The guy was having the same thoughts she was, judging by the way his eyes lingered.

My mind was racing with options. I could fight them, possibly win, considering how others' powers had affected me so far. But we weren't trying to cause problems with law enforcement. Then again, I was standing there stark naked, and this lady had just had her fingers up my ass. If that wasn't fighting business, I wasn't sure what was.

"You can't go—" a voice said, interrupted by a yelp and then the sound of the door swishing open.

There stood Navani and Sacrada, neither being

rude enough to stare other than with the first initial shock.

"What's the meaning of this?" Navani demanded. She stormed up to the woman. "Do you have any idea who he is?"

The woman looked her up and down, then her eyes flickered to Sacrada. "I didn't, until now…"

Before I could even take my next breath, the room exploded with electricity—the man flew back, Navani's eyes blazed blue as shields rose up before her and me. Sacrada was hit, but the impact only infuriated her.

The woman was standing there, hand still sparking, glaring at each of us in turn. "You won't leave this room alive, Earther," she said and turned to point the attack full-on at me this time. Navani and Sacrada moved in for the attack, but so did I.

Just as that first attack in the bank hadn't killed me, this one hit with a force that should have made me shit myself. But I didn't. Instead, I was charging her, the blue lightning flowing over my body. Navani and Sacrada paused in their assault, both amazed at what they were seeing, while the man cursed and pressed back against the wall, taking on the metal of it as his own form of a shield, I imagined. I leaped up, powered by the energy that had come off her attack, and slammed my fist into her. She blocked, but the impact still sent her flying across the room, so that her head smacked against the wall and caved in on itself.

All eyes went to me, and I stumbled forward, catching myself on Navani.

"We need to get out of here, fast," she said, then pointed at the man. "One word of alarm, one person follows us, you're the first one I'm coming after."

His metallic eyes glared at her, but he didn't move from the wall.

"What just happened in there?" Sacrada asked as we ran and she paused to toss me my clothes. The armor morphed and wrapped around me so that by my first step out the door I was fully clothed and ready for action.

"She was working with Ranger, apparently," Navani answered.

We turned down the main hallway and were out into the processing room, where lines of men and women went about their business with paperwork and trading of goods and whatnot. A guard nodded at us, and we slowed, trying to look inconspicuous. When we passed him, Navani said, "Lamb, you might want to get the hell out of there. Now."

There was a commotion, shouting, and an explosion, and then the sight of the ship taking off.

"They didn't like that," Lamb replied. "I'll be hiding out, ready."

As she took off, several ships followed in hot pursuit. At my next step, my legs nearly gave out on me.

"I don't understand," I said, my voice low. "Her powers fueled me, but I'm so weak. I thought... I thought sex and stuff was supposed to give me energy."

"Clearly it's worked itself out by now," Navani said, and Sacrada glanced at us, curiously.

"Yes, but... the woman, she... stuck her fingers... you know."

Navani laughed, in spite of the worry in her eyes. "Were you enjoying it? In the mood for that?"

"I never am," I said, more defensively than I'd meant.

"Exactly. It's not sex exactly that fuels your power. Remember? It's more like the hormones that such deeds activate. You're not feeling them now, in spite of how close we are because you're freaking out. But if I were to...," she took me around the next corner, where there was a drinking fountain, and leaned in, nibbling on my earlobe and said, "...do this, while imagining your cock in my mouth," before pulling back and staring into my eyes. "Well?"

I frowned, confused, but then felt it. A surge of

energy ran through me, similar to the chill I might get, and rush of blood when I was turned on. The result was a slight burst of energy, kind of like a healing of my muscles and fatigue.

"That works?" Sacrada asked.

"I think so," I said.

She gave me a doubtful look, then said, "Well, since we need to get this over with and find my sister... you're going to love this."

This time she stepped forward, placed one hand on my face as her leg moved between mine, her thigh rubbing my crotch. As more energy started to flow into me, she leaned in so that our lips were about an inch apart. I could feel her warm breath on me, and when my chest rose with my heaving breathing, she tilted her head to the side and pressed her breasts against me. "So... working?"

I nodded, breathed out again.

"Teasing works too, apparently," she said with a grin as she pulled away, then glanced at the doors nearby. "We need to hide for a sec. Good timing, because I really need to use the ladies room."

"What?" Navani said. "Didn't you think about that on the ship?"

She shrugged. "Yes, but Lamb offered me some of that energy water you have, and it goes right through me." She pointed behind her, where several guards were moving through the crowd but hadn't spotted us yet. "Come on."

With that, she pulled us both into the ladies room, much to my consternation. I was still feeling the surge of energy from her, while she left us for a stall that looked nothing like what we had back on Earth. Here they had raised platforms with holes at the top, where apparently people were supposed to squat. The walls were like white metal, with a sliding door that went up and down, closing behind her.

"You two check the window for a way out while I take care of this," Sacrada said, and Navani turned to me with a frown.

"Actually," Navani considered me. "Can you pull up your screen this far away from Lamb? I'm not really sure how it works, but I think it should since you have the suit from her."

I tried, and the screen came up. Remembering that only I could see my screen—aside from Lamb when she was around, I nodded. "It's there."

"Good. You did just defeat that lady, after all, and she seemed pretty powerful. Any updates on levels or…?"

I checked, and the percentage bar showed I was very close, but not quite up to the next level yet, which I told her.

"Damn." She went to the window, checking it and

found that it had bars, then turned back, frowning. "Well, keep on it. If we get a chance to go up against anyone else sometime soon, we'll let you do the dirty work to get that next level."

"And if I die in the process?"

"We'll do our best to ensure that doesn't happen."

The toilet flushed, and Sacrada emerged, giving us a nod. "Situation?"

"Bars," Navani said. "Metal."

Sacrada grinned. "I got this." She stepped up next to them, then burst into her glowing golden form. Placing her hands on the bars, they lit up as if about to melt, when suddenly an alarm went off and her powers vanished. The bars were half melted.

She cursed, tried again, but nothing happened.

"We might have that chance to fight much sooner than I'd thought," Navani said, eyes glowing blue as she looked at the walls. "Five of them nearby, converging."

"I don't understand," I admitted.

"Power dampener," Navani explained. "They must have a super nearby that can cancel out attack powers. It wouldn't matter to something like my blue sight, but fire so powerful it can melt metal? You bet it would catch that."

Sacrada looked furious, so furious that she stormed up to me and said, "And his powers? This weird getting stronger thing. Would he be able to break the metal?"

Navani looked confused, then grinned. "Yes, I imagine so."

"Well then, hotshot," Sacrada said, rolling her eyes. She grabbed one of my hands and stuck it into the fold of her suit, moving it so that I cupped her breast. My cock shifted, I gulped, and my hand massaged that perfect, soft breast as I salivated. "Enough?"

"Let him kiss it, see what that does," Navani said. "Quick."

Sacrada gave her a doubtful glance but was in a hurry. She pulled her outfit aside so that her breasts were there for me to see, then said, "Do it."

"I'm not sure this is the best way to—" I started, but she sighed, grabbed me by the back of my head, and thrust my head into her breasts. First, she moved them across my face, then stopped with one cute little, hard nipple brushing against my lower lip.

Hell, I might as well. With full gusto and passion, I leaned into it, bending at the waist to cup her breast and lick it from bottom to nipple, then trace around her aureola before taking her nipple in my mouth and letting my tongue explore it.

She bit her lip and seemed to be trying to fight

the urge to moan, to love what was happening, while my boner pressed uncomfortably against my outfit.

"Now," Navani said.

But neither of us heard. I pulled back, letting my lips suck on her nipple as I did, and then licked across to her other breast as one of my hands started tracing her body, moving down past her ribs, across her hip bone, and then—

BAM! The door slammed open and I processed the fact that Navani had been shouting for us to stop as three guards entered.

"Dammit!" Sacrada said, stepping back and covering her breasts. A sight I would sorely miss.

All I could think about was that these bastards were responsible for that moment of perfection ending, and I wanted to make them pay for it.

They barely had time to process what was happening as I charged into them, tackling the first. I wasn't moving as fast as if I'd had sex, but the hormonal reaction to being able to go to town on Sacrada's breasts was working its magic. My speed and strength were greatly enhanced so that when I leaped up from the first one and kicked out the knee of the next, he fell with a scream and went out as soon as my fist connected with his head. I felt the surge as my power increased from having landed a combo, and turned, ready for more.

The third's eyes flared red, and he pushed his hands forward, lasers shooting out from his palms and hitting the far wall as I dove aside. Navani told Sacrada to let me handle it, and the mere mention of the woman's name sent the sweet taste of her breast back into my mind as I went in for the attack. A woman followed right behind the man, however, so my punch pulled back as I dodged the newcomer's blast of lightning. Apparently, the guards here had a pattern in their powers.

Laser guy tried to turn on me again, but this time I went for the weapon—a quick snap of his wrist and then I took his other arm and broke it, before turning the laser back on the woman.

"Wait," Navani said, shoving me so that the laser hit the door instead, sending a hole through it. "They aren't the bad guys here."

"Someone should tell them that!"

The female guard came at me with a kick to my stomach. I thrust myself backward, but still having a boner, her kick brushed the tip and hurt like hell. She thrust out a hand lit up with more blasts of lightning, and I punched her in the palm of her hand. Bones definitely broke with that punch, and she screamed as she pulled her hand back.

"Get the bars," Sacrada said, moving past me and avoiding eye contact as she went for the lady.

Not wanting to cause any more pain, I slammed my shoulder into the window bars and broke two of them out. Next, I grabbed them, placing my feet against the wall, and yanked. Those two came free also, though that caused me to fall flat on my back with an "Oomph."

"That's enough," Navani said, helping me up as Sacrada returned. A glance showed the female guard was retreating out through door as a wall of flames rose up between her and us.

We all climbed out through the window and found ourselves between two of the tall mobile shield turrets, in a road full of merchants and shoppers, tourists and locals alike. Only one man glanced our way in confusion, but seconds later we were in the crowd, out of harm's way, for now.

I glanced at Navani triumphantly, then to Sacrada.

"Up here," she said, and I realized I'd been focused on her chest.

"Damn, sorry," I mumbled, shaking my head.

"Yeah, well, consider it a one-time thing," she said walking past us to take the lead.

"That was hot," Navani whispered as she leaned into me, taking my arm. "When we find some privacy, me and you. Got it?"

I grinned, certainly turned on enough to, and still

feeling the thrill of the fight. That reminded me. Pulling up the screen, I saw that I'd leveled up and had another skill point to use. When I told her, she said, "Better use it on shields this time. You never know when I won't be around to shield you, and Lamb's suit only holds out so long."

Looking at the shield tree, I bemoaned the fact that I wouldn't be able to get the daze attack I knew my next upgrade on offense would give me, but I also knew she was right. If I were dead, my attack skills wouldn't do any good.

"Ready to go," I said, grinning.

Sacrada glanced back, wondering what we were going on about, and said, "Where's this Threed psychobitch, anyway?"

As Navani showed us the way, I had to worry about whether she was leading a lion to its prey, but kept my mouth shut. Sacrada was a grown woman, she'd have to conduct herself as such if she didn't want to jeopardize the mission. Maybe the prospect of having another woman in my group made me biased, I don't know. But I was growing very excited about meeting said psychobitch.

12

The city was even more fascinating the deeper we got into it. Past the initial defenses we approached an outer ring that was effectively the slums, but beyond that, the city opened up into a series of spiraling and interconnected buildings. In places, it looked like they would fall off and be lost to the rest of the planet, in others they looked strong as an oak, and just as firmly planted.

It was a city of reds and golds, which worked just fine for me. It was like a giant memorial to the Marine Corps, and I could almost imagine those spirals to be the flight paths of Marines as they soared through space. Maybe one of the early settlers here from Earth had been a fellow devil dog?

Whether it was true or not, I liked the idea of it and decided to keep the assumption.

We wound our way down along one of the staircases to an inner sanctum of green, tucked away with its bars and restaurants. The place was throbbing with life. Customers shouted out their orders and waiters and waitresses yelled back, even a couple of children ran past.

"See that?" I said, watching them go by.

"Rare," Sacrada said, watching them with fascination.

"Come to Earth sometime. You'll see more children than you could ever imagine."

"I'd like that," she said, her gold eyes flickering, taking in this place.

"Although, I'm not sure they'd be ready for you," I admitted. "Probably think you're a god or something. Like, a for real god."

"Who are you to say I'm not?" she said with a grin, then followed Navani, who had already started asking around about Threed, inside. She had the image from before displayed on her wrist computer so that it showed up on a small screen on her arm when she held it out. Everyone answered, "No," but we kept trying anyway. After a bit we were growing hungry, so paused for Navani to buy us a vegetable dish wrapped in a thin substance like paper. It was juicy, with a tangy flavor that I quite enjoyed.

"Maybe we're on the wrong planet," I grumbled.

"Or maybe she was finally put in her place," Sacrada said. "Thrown in that horrible prison with the Blue Lady."

"And my brother," I said, frowning.

"Right…"

"On that note, if my brother and she *were* to meet and have a baby, would that fulfill the mission?"

"Considering the fact that they'd be in prison…" Sacrada gave me a doubtful glance.

"Except it sounded like they wouldn't be for long," Navani pointed out. "So, who knows?"

I nodded, for some reason feeling like I was in a race now. I had to hurry up and impregnate one of these women, or my brother would win. The thought was ludicrous, I knew that, but it was still there, driving me forward, making my dick hard again. Damn, how many erections could a man get in one day? Based on all of this so far, quite a lot.

We kept walking as we ate, glancing around, occasionally stopping to ask a bartender, or a passerby if they had seen Threed. Moving out of the main food area, though, Navani glanced back and scrunched her nose.

"What is it?" I asked.

"Someone has been following us for a few minutes, at least," she said. "He's hiding behind the wall there."

"I could go smash his head in," I offered. "Or… try."

"Better to follow my lead," she said, and we all took the next right that we found led into a relatively uncrowded street.

As soon as our stalker turned the corner behind us, we stepped out, ready for anything.

"Why're you looking for her?" the man asked.

He had a strange look to him—a mustache, glasses with an eyepatch over his left eye, and a large hat. A slender fellow.

"You know her?" Navani asked, showing the image.

The man stared at the image, frowning. "Yeah, yeah, I know her. Crazy lady, though that picture does her no justice. She's at least ten times as hot, and a thousand times sexier."

I frowned, noticing the two ladies sharing a confused look.

"Great," I said. "Can you point us to her?"

"Or any information on where she might be," Navani added. "Where she normally hangs out?"

The man held out his hand. "For a price."

Navani considered it, but apparently, that wasn't

Sacrada's style. She lunged forward, grabbing the man's hand, and golden light infused them. Only, before anything could happen, the man was gone, his clothes falling to the ground where he'd been standing just moments ago.

"What the fuck?" I asked, glancing around in confusion. He had literally vanished.

All three of us said it at the same time. "It's her!"

The slender form, the eyepatch covering one eye, the fake mustache on the ground in front of us. It all added up. Spinning quickly, Navani's eyes glowed blue, and she pointed to a ledge above.

"Up there," she shouted, and already Sacrada had her wings spread, taking off for the ledge above.

I started running but paused long enough to see Navani grabbing some of the woman's belongings from where they had fallen.

"You can track her!" I exclaimed, having nearly forgotten about that power of Navani's.

"You bet your ass I can," she said, eyes glowing brighter than usual as she held up the item and scanned the area around us. "This way," she said as she took off, barely slowing to see if I was staying with her.

The sounds of fighting came from above, and then a woman went flying over the edge, only to disappear a second later.

"Another replica," Sacrada shouted as she appeared, flying out.

"It's okay, we've got her," Navani replied, ducking into a tunnel that led down and underneath the green part of the city. What else could I do but follow?

Navani was moving fast, scaling a wall with that purple energy like I'd seen her do earlier, and then pushing herself to even greater speeds. I wasn't completely powerless here, and now that I had leveled up again I felt extra support from my suit, like an advanced exoskeleton that gives more push to each movement. It wasn't much, but every little bit helped, as she was quickly losing me.

I didn't want to call out for her to stop, so I kept on as best I could. It was only when I had found myself deep within the city's depths with no sign of her that I began to worry. A canal ran to my left, tall bridges overhead creating darkness around me.

As luck would have it in these dark areas, I noticed several men and women leering at me, and a couple started to approach. Dammit, I didn't want any trouble, not with them. They were laughing, pointing, and then I saw why. It wasn't just at me, but what was in the canals, with me walking so close and unaware. A strange creature watching, salivating. It had just poked its head up, looking to be somewhere between a human and an alligator. I had to wonder if this was some sort of super-related mutation, or perhaps a genetic modification. Alien life forms likely existed, but we hadn't come across any so human-like so far.

"Careful there, Utopu," one of the women said. "It's as likely to bite your ass off as not, and with a cute little tush like that, it'd be a waste."

I took a step toward them, but a man in a gray cloak came and threw up a hand so that I hit an invisible barrier.

The creature behind me was approaching, apparently sensing my new predicament. Again I lunged to get away, but the super grinned, that wall still there. Something told me that these supers weren't on the hero side.

"Get out of my way," I growled.

"Who's in your way," the super asked, gesturing to the path ahead, following the canal. "Nobody's in your way, sir. If you're lost, keep on walking, I'm sure you can find yourself a guide."

"I'm not looking for a fight," I warned them. "My friends are very powerful…"

They laughed at that. "He's got powerful friends," one jeered. Another threw a rock at me and laughed when it hit the invisible barrier and clattered to the ground.

It almost covered the sound of water sloshing. Now that I got a good look at the thing coming at me, I was certain it had to have been a product of some sort of genetic modification. It was covered in scales, dripping water from its long tail and, moved with power and a lack of humanity in its eyes.

"Guys," I said, backing away from it. "I have a mission here, it's extremely important that I—" My back hit the barrier, giving them another reason to laugh. And then the beast charged.

I still had some energy in me, I thought, so I braced myself. It was fast, coming in with its tail swinging and then opening its mouth wide. But I had my ladies to get back to, a new one to find, and new strength and speed from leveling up that I wanted to test out.

His tail caught me off guard, but it also used up his focus. With a superman punch, I landed the first blow, only to get knocked off my feet by his tail when it whipped at me again. The next blow was a double fist, raised and then brought back down on me. My shield absorbed some of the hit, but it was meant for projectiles, not this. When he went to strike again, I rolled out of the way and remembered the strategy. Quick, combo hits. I caught his arm with an uppercut, leaped over the tail and kicked it, then moved right so that my next two punches took it in the hard, scaly part of its back. I didn't' care one bit that my hands were bloodied, I had my bonus, and the strikes were coming harder and faster. My next punch took him on the shoulder and actually tore his scaly skin.

When he tried to trip me again, I slammed my foot down on his tail and earned more bonus strength, so that not only was his tail smashed, but my punch for his stomach broke right through, leaving him to stumble back with an imprint of my fist as proof of what I'd just done.

The crowd was staring at me in horror now, half starting to goad each other into attacking me, while others were already starting to back up into the shadows.

"Nah, this guy ain't super," the gray-cloaked man said. "Just lucky."

"Try me then," I said and stepped into a punch toward him. The red energy from before formed, ending in a sonic-boom type blast of air that shattered the barrier put up by the man.

That sent the rest of them running, all but the man in gray. He charged me, flashing barriers appearing before him as he did, pushing me back toward the water, but between strikes I lifted my fist and sent it into the ground.

It should've hurt, it should've crushed my bones,

but I was so amped up that instead it tore into the ground and sent a shockwave at him. He fell back, stunned, and then I was on him. This motherfucker had tried to kill me! As much as I hated the idea of death, I'd come to be the bastard's friend in the Marines. It was time I sent him another soul.

Only a few strikes later, and I was feeling better, satisfied with his bloody state. Whether he was alive or dead, he certainly wouldn't be causing anyone problems anytime soon.

I glanced up to see two more of them watching, and I took a step to attack. Only, when they emerged from the shadows, I could see that they were only children.

"How... how did you do that?" the taller of them asked. "I mean... could you do it again?"

"Get out of here," I said, frustrated that they would be in the way of danger and that I'd almost gone after them.

"The one there..." the boy indicated the abomination, "the alligator men, there are more. They hunt us."

"Kill them," the other boy said. "Please."

I frowned, not knowing how to deal with this situation. "I've lost my friends. I really need to find them."

"We can help you," that tall boy said, lighting up

—literally. His eyes lit up blue, like Navani's. "We know our way around this place, and I can see things others can't."

This was the hero stuff I had always dreamed about. Why I joined the Space Marines in the first place. It certainly hadn't been to fly around shooting at other Marines in the stupid political battles of the Elites of Paradise Planets, as had ended up being the case. Had I been a hero then? By their definition, sure. But here, actually helping kids against crazy alligator mutations? While I had my own mission to get to, I hadn't a clue as to where the ladies were or how to find them.

I laughed, then nodded. "Lead the way."

The boys' faces lit up, and they scampered off, with me close behind.

"They like to hang out around the inner core," one of them called over his shoulder as if I would have any idea what that meant. "Picking on us… sometimes making one of us go missing."

There wasn't much doubt in my mind what that meant, and it cemented my desire to see the mutations pay.

13

The boys led me back through the green part of town, then down and around to a new set of canals. We had been going too far, running for too long, and I was definitely worried about the mission with Navani and the sisters.

"Where is this place?" I asked again but then saw my answer.

Two of those alligator creatures were hovering over a corpse. An instant sickness took over, and I couldn't hold back. I charged forward, not quite processing what the boys were shouting, that this was a typical trap—until it was too late.

I pulled back to punch, as the alligator creatures spun around and came at me, two more leaping out from buildings at my sides. Each of them grabbed me and threw me to the ground before I had a chance to react, and then fell on me with mouths open ready for the kill.

My Marine training kicked in—years of grappling with the boys—and I shifted down below one and rotated out to get to the outside, shoving this one into his friend. A tail lashed out and caught me across the back of my head so that I saw stars.

The boys were shouting, my own little cheerleaders, and I was reminded that I couldn't let them down.

My combo punch strategy worked fine against one or two opponents, but I quickly saw that it was tougher when fighting four alligator mutants. As soon as I'd land two hits, one of them would strike, knocking off my combo. At one point they had me up against a wall, and one of them managed to get his teeth on my shoulder—luckily, my biotech armor was in full effect, and his teeth created a sickening, scraping sound.

The others backed off slightly at that, and I saw my opening. With a one-two combo to the one, I came in for a hook to the next one's body, then an uppercut to the jaw. The first was back at me, but I ran at him, thrusting my arm into his mouth and created that scraping sound again as the armor hit teeth.

It worked! They all cringed, and I had another shot. A kick to the legs, an ax kick to finish one off, and then I was in my zone. The pattern was simple—combo strikes, teeth grind, combo strikes. Two fell, then a third, and the fourth ran.

I gave chase, catching him by the tail and slamming him face-first into the pavement.

When he turned over, I was there, fist pulled back.

"One time, I'll tell you," I warned him. "Leave my friends alone." With that, I nodded to the boys.

"Of course," he said, voice rough, mangled.

"Tell your friends."

I stood and released him. The boys ran over, talking about 'did you see that' and 'wow, how amazing,' and whatnot. I was just glad to have had the chance to do something heroic. It felt like something straight out of the legends.

"What next?" I asked, glancing around, ready for more action.

"Maybe teach us some of your moves?"

I grinned. "Okay, find us a safe spot. I'll at least go over the basics, though it won't do much good against their type. If you practice every day, spar with each other, become better fighters... who knows."

"Plus, I can do this," one of the boys said, and he grinned as spikes shot out from his back, like a damn porcupine. "Helps at least keep them off of me."

"And you?" I asked the other boy, having nearly forgotten that they were supers too.

"It's nothing, really," he admitted. "Only..." He touched the nearby metal building and, for a few seconds after letting go, his fists became that same metal. "There are various styles of supers," he said. "I'm one of those who can take on the properties of objects I touch."

What he said made me think, questioning if maybe my absorption of powers was somehow related. Not that it mattered.

"Well, both of your powers will come in handy in a fight," I said, as we reached the spot they were leading me to. "Now, take up a stance like this, fists up."

For the next thirty minutes or so, we went through the basics of the Marine Corps Martial Arts program or MCMAP. "Sounded as spelled, not with each letter individually," I told them when they asked what it was all about, where I'd learned this. From the greatest warriors to ever live.

It wasn't much, but if they kept it up, it would be

something. I had just taken a stance to show them some more advanced anti-knife techniques when something hit my shoulder. I turned to see that it had been a rock, and glanced around, expecting to see more kids maybe.

"Dammit, Drew!" The voice came from above, and I looked up to see Navani standing there, Sacrada walking up to her side. "If you'd been lost, or dead... the whole mission would've been done for!"

"Unless it's already worked," I pointed out. "It's not like anyone's been tested yet."

She shook her head, confused, as the two of them approached. "No, Lamb does instant testing. It's a simple scan. Sorry, not out of this yet."

"Darn," I said with a laugh, then turned to my two guides. "These boys helped me out." In a way they had, in that they gave me the opportunity to feel like a hero, to gain more experience, and to see that there were actual children on these planets. Maybe baby-making wasn't as complicated as Navani seemed to think.

"Well, there's not much we can do to repay the favor but..." Navani held up her scanner and ran it across them, then smiled. "There you go. Tell the vendors at the food booths you're covered."

"A meal?" the shorter one asked, eyes lighting up.

"Not *a* meal," she replied. "Forever. Meals for life, or as long as the Citadel's funding is intact. You're covered."

Both of them stared, their eyes wide, and the taller mumbled his appreciation.

"That was kind," I said as we left them behind.

"It was the least I could do, considering that they babysat you while we were taking care of business."

"I didn't need babysitting—oh, you found Three?"

"We did and paid off some locals to watch her until we get back," Sacrada explained.

I followed them along to the upper levels and a restaurant, where we had to descend the stairs into a place that almost felt like a dungeon. A central path went through the restaurant, with each dining area divided up as its own room. There were no doors, but curtains on the sides of each doorway.

Outside one of these, three supers were standing in suits, holding up barriers while a woman waited inside. One look at that pink hair flipped to the side, and those eyes—one red, one blue—and I knew we had our lady.

"Wait, so I missed all the drama?" I asked.

"Does that make you sad?" Sacrada asked, a hint of annoyance in her voice. "You wanted to watch a cat fight?"

"No, I was just… curious."

"Let's say we aren't good, but it's not going to distract us from saving my sister."

"Fine."

Navani paid the guys off, and they exited, leaving us to step into the room with Threed. "About damn time," Threed said.

"We had to find our friend," Navani explained.

"Now," Sacrada added.

"Wait," Threed replied, eyeing me with those crazy eyes. "So this is… this is him?"

"That's right," Navani said.

Threed licked her lips, then walked up to me, eyeing me like an outfit at a clothing store as she circled me.

"Yeah, I could get into this, or, you know." She grinned at me and slid the top half of her outfit off, then shimmied out of it so that she was standing there in just her long gloves and boots.

"We don't have time for this," Sacrada growled.

"Actually," Navani countered, looking at her holo-screen. "I've given Lamb our location, and she has to come get us. While we're in a rush, we don't want the entire city after us, so… she's going to be stealthy."

"Meaning?"

"We have a little time."

Sacrada clenched her jaw, but leaned back, accepting it.

"Let's save the galaxy, big boy," Threed said with an even wider smile. She stood with her arms behind her head, moving her hips seductively. "Isn't that what we're doing here?"

Navani glanced around, nervously. "Um, so you're familiar with the prophecy?"

"You're calling it that now?" Sacrada asked with a hint of scorn.

"No, I mean because you did…" Navani glared, turned back to Threed, and waited for a response.

"Fuck yeah I am," Threed said, already walking over to me, pushing me back into one of the chairs, and starting to rub her bare ass against my crotch. "I've been waiting for this shit for forever. Saving myself for this day."

"*You* are a virgin?" Sacrada scoffed.

"I didn't say that," Threed said. "I said saving myself, you know, like not dying. Saving my life instead of taking it or letting others take it… so that I could do my part for the galaxy."

At that, she turned around and pouted, then grabbed my cock. Hard. "Why isn't it erect?"

"I'm a little caught off guard," I admitted.

She rolled her eyes, then undid my outfit and pulled out my limp dick. As hot as this might have been with more privacy, I was feeling very awkward here and now very exposed. She started trying to jack me off, then groaned.

"Great, you guys bring me the guy, and he can't even get it up!" She let it flop in her hand, then knelt down between my legs. "Maybe it just needs a little help."

"Or maybe it can wait," I said.

She frowned. "He's gay?"

"I'm not gay."

Ignoring me, she turned to Navani. "What's wrong with him?"

"I think you're just coming on a bit strong," Navani said, trying not to laugh now. "Maybe if we get out of here…"

Several customers walked by, all looking over in disgust at Threed kneeling naked in front of me, flapping my dick around.

"Ugh, why's everyone else in the world such prudes?" Threed said, standing and starting to dress again.

"Sorry," I said. "Maybe you have a place we can regroup, then… get to the mission? Work into it a bit?"

She scrunched her nose like she'd just bit into a lemon, but nodded. "Yeah, come on, everyone. You can even tell that whore Sacrada she can come.

Maybe we can make up sexually. Always the best way, if you ask me."

At the mention of that, my dick started to grow slightly, but I tucked it away as I followed. Threed glanced over though, noticing my action. She seemed thoughtful, then winked.

14

W e were passing a large dome in the center of the city, what looked like some sort of arena, when half a dozen men and a couple of women noticed Threed and called out after her, grabbing sticks and bats and running over to apparently bash her skull in.

The rest of us stared in confusion, but she took off running. The group didn't pay us any attention as they gave chase.

"We can't lose her again so soon," Navani said.

"Can't we?" Sacrada looked hopeful, but Navani shook her head.

"Fine," Sacrada said. "But I'm not saving her ass."

"What part of teamwork do you not understand?"

Navani challenged, but growled and ran after the gang instead of waiting for an answer.

I gave Sacrada an *I'm-so-let-down* look and charged after Navani. By the time we caught up with them, though, they had Threed, holding her against a wall and punching her in the gut. One of the men stepped forward and slammed her upside the head with his metal stick, and when he pulled back, one of her eyes was smattered with blood. It was horrific, disgusting.

And... I realized as I heard a laugh from behind, not her at all. It was a replica! Again.

The others all turned at that, cursing at the sight of her appearing with a blaster that she unleashed. Three of them fell before the others could get to her, and now we were in the fight too. One of them had this really weird leaping ability, where he'd basically leap over our heads to attack from the other side, thinking it was the best thing ever. On his second leap, I caught him with a back kick to the gut that sent him right into his buddy, who had blades for fingers and, when trying to catch his friend ended up killing him instead.

The blade-fingered guy let out a scream and came at me, but I threw myself out of his way, taking a hit from a metal bar in the process, but only to the shoulder. It clanged against my armor, and I spun as

I landed an elbow to his face, taking him down before turning back and finishing off another.

Navani was dodging strikes left and right, and I got the feeling her blue sight allowed for a bit of being able to see where they'd come from next, because there was no way she could simply be *that* good.

Threed came back in with two replicas, and soon we had them on the run. All but the main one who had first struck Threed's replica. Navani slammed him to the ground, then pinned him down with her boot.

"What did she do?" Navani asked.

"Made a run against us," the man said. "Took the entire lending house down, then tried to start her own."

"They were corrupt," Threed mumbled in her defense, still a bit out of it. "It was my civic duty."

"Bullshit," the man said. "She's as rotten as the rest of us.

Navani considered him, then let go. "Get out of here. If you come back around her, you're dead. Hear me?"

He grumbled but ran off.

"You've got skeletons to get rid of," Navani said to Threed.

"You have no idea," Threed said, then motioned

for us to follow. "Come on, the house is this way. Let's get rested up."

"Is there somewhere my ship can land nearby to get us out of here?" Navani asked. "We've lingered too long already."

"A field out back," Threed replied. "Don't worry about it."

We didn't have much farther to walk before reaching the house. She had still been rubbing her stomach from where they'd been hitting her replica, which gave me new questions to consider regarding how her replica system worked. It stopped when we arrived. She smiled, held out a hand in a gesture of welcome, and said, "Isn't she grand?"

It was a dome with alternating metal and stone, built up in a way that reminded me of something between a castle and the old twenty-first-century style mansions shown in videos of how life used to be on Earth. Like a primitive but equally decadent home on one of the Paradise Planets. Tall windows lined the upper floors, a large arched roof giving it the feel of a hunting lodge. It was all over the place, yet perfect for someone like Threed... in an unbelievable sense.

"How the fuck do you live here?" Sacrada said, jealousy clear in her voice. I was reminded of her little apartment where we'd found her.

"Should a goddess live in anything less?" Threed replied. "A girl finds a way to make do. It so happens, I can easily work three jobs at once."

Had she winked at me when she said that? It happened so fast, I wasn't sure.

"It's amazing," I said. "Back on Earth, these places don't even exist anymore. Not this big, definitely not this nice."

"Come on in," she said. "I'll give you the tour."

She showed us around the outer halls, to the large statues of famous supers on this planet, and even a massive painting of what the ruins of Melatand had looked like before they were ruins. A city straight out of legend—one truly built for the gods.

"What's the status on Lamb?" Sacrada asked, growing more impatient.

"Inbound," Navani said. "Goros is waiting out there for us. We'll get him."

"Easier said when your sister isn't being held hostage," Sacrada said, then turned and stormed off.

"Where are you going?"

"To fucking unwind," Sacrada said, not even turning. "I need to calm down, and it's that or punch someone in the face."

We all watched her go, then Threed excused herself to check on something. Navani and I went to the kitchens, and she asked me all about Earth. She couldn't understand how we'd let it get so bad, or how the elitist system of the Paradise Planets had been allowed to happen. Worst of all was when I got to the topic of Planet Kill—the live streaming reality show of people who volunteered to compete for a chance to ascend. She quickly changed the subject, a look of sickness coming over her.

"I don't know," she said, rummaging through the cupboards. "I just always thought Earth was this grand place. The land the legends speak of is nothing like how you describe it."

"It's changed over the years, that's for sure."

"Our galaxy will too if Ranger has his way." She looked over her shoulder at me. "We, and by that I mean you, can't let that happen."

"I'm doing my best," I said. "What with the fighting and fucking, I mean, what else do you want of me?"

She frowned, clearly not having an answer. "Sorry if I'm not sounding grateful. I know, it must be so hard to be expected to let us worship your cock like this."

"That's not fair," I said. "Is it a dream come true? In many ways, yes. But come on, Threed?"

"You don't think she's attractive?"

"Is this some sort of test?" I waited, watching for any signs of jealousy.

"Drew, if I was jealous, which maybe I'll be from time to time, who knows... would allowing it to show help the mission? No. So if you find her in the least bit sexy, great. If not, we still need this to happen. Imagine Sacrada if you need to."

"Maybe I'll imagine you, instead."

She cringed. "Was that supposed to somehow sound flattering? Romantic?"

"I see now how it might not."

"At least you're not a complete idiot." She turned back with a laugh, bending over to search the lower cupboards. Her outfit clung to her ass, and I couldn't help but stare. If I needed to imagine something to make it happen, that image right there would definitely be it.

She stood to see me adjusting myself, and said, "Nuts."

"What?"

She held up a jar of nuts in one hand, dried fruit in the other. "Found some nuts, as I see you did too."

My hand was still on my crotch, I realized, and I quickly moved it and put it in my pocket. We moved to the table, and she gave me a sly grin.

"I'm surprised you try to hide it at all, now," she said. "That boner of yours pops up so often, I wonder if there's something medically wrong with you."

"On Earth, we don't just let them out whenever they pop up, you know. And I don't know, it seems like something to hide until it's time to use it."

"Well, don't feel like you need to hide it from me. I like it, after all."

I laughed at that, accepting some food. She checked on Lamb and cursed.

"Another delay," Navani explained. "Seems the locals are on high alert, thanks to our entrance into the city."

"Sorry."

She laughed. "Comes with the territory."

As we waited, the conversation moved to the topic of our worlds, about Earth and my early days in the Marines, about how I felt when I first went into space, and how I knew it was my home. She thought that idea was cute, explaining that she'd actually been born *and* conceived on spaceships, spent a few years of her teenage life on a space station studying the effects of their sun on supers, trying to understand why the sun gave some of them powers like it did, but not all people. As far as they'd been able to tell, it was related to certain blood types and DNA, and the way those interacted with the sun's radiation.

I found it all fascinating, but when she started getting into the more scientific aspects of it, I found myself tuning out, my eyes moving down to her lips, her cleavage… the smooth line of her neck, just below her ears.

Just when I was pretty sure I was going to nod off and had started having fantasies that bordered on dreams, Threed walked in and stood there with her silly grin.

"You ready?" she asked, then gestured me to follow. I checked with Navani, but she shooed me off.

"You're… sure about this?" I asked Navani.

"Hell, I got mine," she said. "And honestly, I'm still a bit sore. Go tear someone else up, will you."

I laughed and nodded, following Threed. An escape from the science talk was certainly welcome, and Threed wasn't bad to look at. The woman's tattoos were sexy as hell, but maybe a bit intimidating. It didn't make sense—I'd slept with my fair share of female Marines. I liked my women tough. Maybe it was that this particular woman bordered on insane that worried me.

"Where are we going?" I asked.

"Oh, you'll love it," Threed replied. She led me up some stairs, then around to a curving hall, and finally into a room to the right. The lighting was dark, but she'd lit a couple of scented candles—fresh rain, was my best guess, though I didn't imagine they had that exact scent. There were large windows along the inner wall, looking in on a bath. We had cushions, couches, and even a bed.

She reclined on one of the cushions, folding her legs like a lady, and looked at me. "You know, half of this is just for show."

"The house?"

"No, silly." She laughed a girly, playful giggle. "This persona, who I am. It's all part of the act, baby."

"Oh, so you're not really crazy."

"I am, definitely. But what I'm saying is I *know* I'm crazy, and I'm okay with it. As I accept it more, I get crazier. It's a fun cycle. Problem is, I'm so often misjudged, mislabeled."

I wasn't so sure of that. "Did you steal Sacrada's man?"

"Stealing isn't really the right word."

"How's that?"

"Well, don't you know who we are?" She uncrossed her legs, leaning in, eyes looking crazy again. "We're gods."

"I don't think that's accurate."

"Ex-gods, to be precise," she said. "Our parents were gods. We would've been gods, had it not all fallen apart. So, what, a god should limit herself to one mortal man? Another god should be able to claim these men?"

"I'm sorry, but… you do know you were never *actually* a god, right? Or immortal?"

She laughed, brushing her hand across my arm as she said, "You're so silly."

It wasn't an answer, not really. And yet, in spite of her craziness, or maybe kind of because of it, I found myself kinda liking her.

"I've never really been the type to be with more than one woman at a time," I admitted.

She grinned. "I did. Three women once, actually, but just because some guy I really liked was watching. Turned out, he wanted the blonde. Always the fucking blonde. And no, it wasn't Sacrada, as much fun as that would've been."

"And this? Now?" I shifted uncomfortably. "Are you going to be part of this, and still be off screwing around?"

She laughed again, this time loud. "Honey, you're so sweet. You want to be my boyfriend? I accept. We'll all be your little girlfriends in this harem thingy. Harem Guardians of the Universe or some shit, right?" She shook her head, grinning, and I couldn't tell if she was mocking me or really into it.

She stood, stretching so that the light from the candles danced across her curves, playing with her cleavage and casting a dark shadow between her legs. An enticing view, for sure.

"This is how you'll seduce me?" I asked with a laugh. Hell, it was starting to work. She stood there with her curvy body silhouetted against the bright light beyond, and her smile seemed almost like that of a normal person.

"Turn around," she said, pulling me out of my seat. "Stand up and turn around."

Okay, back to her weird side. "I'm not super into any of that kinky stuff."

"Shut up and just… look behind you."

I did, turning to the windows, and then froze there, my breath caught. Walking out from beneath us, toward the waters, was Sacrada in a silk robe. She paused, looked around, and then slowly let the robe fall from her shoulders. Her bare backside was exposed, nothing but flesh. Her golden hair fell down to the middle of her back, just above the point where the curve of her hips started. Oh, that ass. It was definitely one worth writing home about.

Threed stepped up behind me, wrapping her hands around to my chest, the other feeling my abs. "She won't let you have her yet, will she."

"No," I admitted.

"But I will." Threed's hands moved along the

inner lining of my pants, taunting me. "And she never has to know we were watching."

"That's…"

"Wrong?" She reached down, fingers playing with my hair, brushing against the base of my cock. "I know, it's so, so… wrong."

As wrong as I knew it was, my eyes couldn't leave the image of Sacrada, now at the edge of the bath, dipping her toe in. I saw that the other side of the wall had mirrors on it, and I figured that's what she saw if she looked up at us.

Sacrada lowered herself into the water, turning slightly so that I saw the outline of her breast, and then Threed was in, and hands were rubbing my hard cock, finding my balls, exploring me.

"That's more like it," Threed said, and then she began undressing me. I started to turn to her, but she grinned and moved my face away again, saying, "Watch."

So I did, hands pressed up against the glass as Threed jacked me off from behind. Only, then she was on her knees in front of me, and I *wanted* to look at her.

It was still somewhat dark in here, and the oddness of her eyes wasn't noticeable. I ran a hand through her pink hair as she slid my cock into her mouth. Then, I don't know if it was all the built-up tension or the fact that I was seeing Sacrada bathing at the same time, but as soon as her warm, moist mouth surrounded me, I couldn't help myself. She stroked me once, twice, and then my legs felt like they were on fire, my balls pulling up as my abs clenched and my hips rocked back as I came.

She tried to pull back, but it caught her on the cheek, cum dripping down her hand as she did her best to move out of the way and failing miserably. The final shot hit her on the forehead as she tried to go the other way to escape, and I was standing there, hands still pressed to the glass, her glaring up at me with cum all over her face.

"The fuck?" she said.

"At least you did a good job," I said, trying to be helpful.

"I know. I did a *damn* good job. Shit. Next time, why don't you try and do your part?"

Her eyes actually looked more let down than angry, as she stood, wiped it off, and then turned and walked away. I was left standing there, all by myself, staring down at Sacrada in the bath. The guilt of the situation hit me, and now in addition to being embarrassed about cumming too soon, I was left feeling like a peeping pervert.

Down below, Threed appeared, walking to the baths, nude, and she gestured up toward me. Sacrada looked up, shrieked, and got out of the water, storming off. Oh no. Sure enough, when I looked up at what had been mirrors on the opposite side, I saw now windows.

That crazy bitch had shut off the mirror side and shown me, standing like that staring down at Sacrada with a half-limp dick.

Yeah, my chances with the woman were fading fast.

All I could do was rub my head to try to fight off the headache that was starting to form, and wonder how I was going to explain this to Sacrada. Next on my plate would be dealing with Threed and getting her on my side.

Since she was looking up at me and laughing, I wasn't sure how easy that was going to be. Maybe if I gave her a good lay, the craziness would fade. Right now, though, she was the last thing I felt like doing.

15

The mood was dark when I entered the grand foyer, where Navani and Sacrada sat, glaring at me.

"Navani, can I have a word with Sacrada?" I asked.

"I... think it's safer if I stay here."

"Safer...?" A look at the expression on Sacrada's face, and I saw what she meant. "Okay, here goes. I didn't mean for that to happen. I didn't plan—"

"To invade my privacy like that?" Sacrada spat back, standing now and getting in my face. "You think because I let you lick my tits, you get to watch me bathe while you whack it like a horny teenager, you pervert."

"Shit." I stared, unable to think of what else to say. "Shit."

"Do better," Navani said. "Maybe the truth."

With a sigh, I told them what had happened. They stared up at me with a mixture of anger and amusement, and then finally Sacrada said, "Threed... I should've known. Still, you could've looked away."

"I could have," I admitted. "I should have. You just don't understand. Imagine you're looking into the sky and the clouds open up, and there's heaven in all its glory, and God warned you not to look, but it's there, right in front of you. Heaven!"

"Laying it on a bit thick," Navani hissed.

"Go on," Sacrada said, holding up a hand.

"I mean it, looking at you, at both of you... I mean, I was with attractive women back home, but you two are goddesses in my eyes. To think that Navani, you slept with me, wow! And Sacrada, when I saw you walk out there, my mind kept saying to look away, but my hormones and everything inside of me said I had to keep looking so that when the sight went away, I would never forget its beauty. I know, that sounds horrible, but—"

"You might see it again," Sacrada said with a tilt to her head.

"What?" I asked.

"Huh?" Navani chimed in.

Sacrada allowed a smile at the corner of her lips. "Keep talking like that, we'll see."

So she liked this idea of someone worshipping her, huh? I could certainly do that. I opened my mouth, but she stopped me.

"After we save my sister," she added.

"Understood," I said with a nod and grinned at Navani, who was giving me a proud smile. Somehow, I'd undone the damage Threed had caused.

"Speak of the devil," Sacrada said, her frown returning.

Turning, I saw that Threed had just entered, wearing only her towel with her outfit slung over her shoulder. She tossed it to the ground and started drying right there, eyeing me, laughing.

"This guy," she said. "I'd say let's have another go, but the owners of this house are right outside. Just saw them on the security cams, so... we should probably get going."

"Owners?" I asked, feeling a horrible sinking in my gut.

"Threed, really?" Navani shook her head, while Sacrada stood and headed for a window.

"She's right," Sacrada said. "It looks like quite a few of them, too, coming back from a party, maybe?"

"What made you think it was mine?" Threed

asked. "Did I explicitly say that? Pssh, I just came to a party here once or twice. Great place."

"Get dressed," Navani commanded Threed. "We're running out of here, and when this is all over, I'm going to slap the stupid out of you."

Threed licked her lips and stuck out her ass, giving it a little slap. "Right here, sugar."

We all ignored that, standing ready to be on our way. Lucky for us, Lamb reported in right then that she was ready if we needed to hightail it out of there. We certainly did.

"Don't attack them," Navani said as we ran down the hall. "That's an order! We're in their house, and we're heroes, dammit."

"Most of us," Sacrada added with a glare in Threed's direction.

"Bite me."

"Oh, I just might."

I wasn't sure if that came out right, but was more focused on the two supers who had just entered through the door in front of us. We retreated toward the rear of the house, where the hall took us toward the upper part, on a hill. Still, enemy was showing up outside, either tracing our location or simply more showing up.

"Intruders, Wing B-5," one of them shouted, and Navani cursed. Threed ran forward, there was a green flashing light, and then there were three of her, engaging in combat. Her replicas hit just as hard as she did, and soon she had one down, the other held in front of her. She reached back with a fist and pulled a green light from the air.

"NO!" Navani shouted, lunging forward and throwing Three off of him—the replicas vanished and the man stumbled forward before falling with a groan. "What did I just say?"

"I'm not getting caught for your morals," Three replied, shoving her off.

"Get us a way out of here," Navani said to Sacrada. "And watch *her*. She tries anything, you have my permission to treat her like the villain she's making me think she is."

"Villain?" Threed scoffed. "This far away from the Citadel, babe, it's a fine line."

"Not anymore," Navani replied, and joined me in watching as Sacrada flew down the hall, giving us space.

That angel of a woman released her wings as a blinding light filled the passage, and we were forced to look away. Heat surged, and there was an explosion, followed by her shouting for us to hurry our asses.

We took off after her, still seeing sunspots. She was out through the hole she had just made, directing her bright light at a group of supers below. A man thrust up and metal cables shot from his wrists to catch her, but she spun, wings cutting them down. The man below shouted in agony, as if his fingers had been severed.

Navani helped me down, while Threed created replicas that took turns jumping down to high-risk areas and catching her, tossing her to the next replica, and then vanishing before they could fall, only to reappear below and help her down to the next. It was a very complicated game of falling leapfrog.

When we reached the bottom, Navani turned to her. "Get another Sacrada up there to fend them off while we retreat."

"One of her is enough," Threed replied, already sprinting off. "No thanks!"

"Maybe Sacrada was right about her," Navani said. We had no choice but to follow, and I certainly couldn't argue. The fact was that this woman was certainly a loose cannon. More like a stick of dynamite about to blow, disguised to look like a cannon.

I glanced back to see that Sacrada was now following but doing so in an arc around to our right as she tried to lead the two supers following her off course. The hole in the house behind us was substantial, and I had to wonder if that made us villains, to a certain degree. Maybe there was some wisdom in what Threed had said? We'd had to take down several guards—though at least we didn't kill the ones who we hadn't known to be on Ranger's side. It'd been close, and that worried me.

And now this.

What the hell was I doing up here, I had to wonder for the billionth time. Here I was, running around like some sort of hero, while in reality, I was causing trouble and just trying to get my dick wet. Fuck.

Wind flew around us as Lamb pulled the ship up nearby, and soon we were piling in. Shots from behind rang out, but the shields protected us. As she took off, she left the ramp open. Within thirty seconds or so, Sacrada came barreling in. Her wings folded in around her, but the gold glow didn't die down. She marched over to Threed and punched her, hard, right across the jaw.

Threed collapsed, instantly. She tried to stand up, stumbled, and then split into three again. Both of her replicas moved for Sacrada, but her focus was off and one faded out while Sacrada broke the neck of the second. It was strange, watching what could have been Threed as far as I knew... dying.

At least that calmed Sacrada, and as she stared at

the corpse that slowly faded away, she said, "Sorry, I didn't... I... I lost control."

Threed—the real one—stared up at her, glaring, and tried to stand again but couldn't. That must have been some punch. I definitely didn't want to take sides, but couldn't sit by and let an injured party of our team go unaided. Nobody said a word when I stepped forward and helped Threed to stand.

"Come on, let's get you a seat. Let this pass."

She wrapped her arms around me, letting me help her walk, and we started off toward the jungle room. It was calming, peaceful. The best place for something like this.

"When she's done, send her my way," Navani called after me. "I need to have a talk with her."

"Roger that," I said, and we went through the sliding doors to the next hallway. Soon we were entering the jungle room, and she looked around in awe, her red eye twitching slightly.

"What is this place?" she asked.

"Reminds me of what Earth supposedly used to look like," I replied, lowering her to the simulated moss floor.

She sat there, legs curled up to her chest, and stared at the moss. The expression in her face was out of place—sorrow, perhaps?

"Are you okay?" I asked.

She shook her head. "It's all fucked up, isn't it? I mean, I'm fucked up. Maybe it's the replica thing, I don't know, like splitting like that one too many times has messed with my head." She looked up at me now, hopeful. "I'm trying though, or... I will. I will try."

"Threed..."

"You believe me, don't you?"

I considered, then nodded. Whether I did or not, at least at this moment I wanted to. We needed her, and hell, we had a bit of a bond going already. The type of bond that comes from getting a blowjob, but still.

"Is it true, about you... getting power from it?" she asked.

I nodded. "As far as I know. It's like I get a boost, depending on how much the activity sets off my hormones, but is still kind of a mystery."

"And we're riding off to battle, I suppose?"

I nodded again.

"Well then." She shrugged, not shy about looking me up and down. "Think you can last this time?"

The proposition seemed so out of nowhere, I had to take a moment to follow, but then said, "We don't have to. I mean, you're going through a lot."

She allowed a smile—a genuine, not-so-crazy

smile, and moved toward me on all fours. "Oh, believe me. I want to."

"You're… sure?"

She nodded, stopping to kneel in front of me. "Payday," she said as she licked her lips, face inches from my crotch. Her mismatched eyes, one blue and one red, stared up at me as she worked to remove my pants. Her other hand was already caressing my cock through my sensation-enabled armor, so that when she accomplished her mission and then removed my boxer-briefs, my pal reported for duty, ready to go.

There was a hint of a smile on her face as she traced her lips with the tip of my cock, one hand gripping it by the base as her other ran along my ass. "Want more?" she said, and then she blinked, creating a copy of herself at my side.

Her replica immediately joined in, Threed moving out of the way but bringing my cock with her. When she engulfed it, I thought I was in heaven. Then her replica's tongue met my balls. My stomach muscles clenched, a tingling worked its way up from my shins to my groin, and I had to bite my lip to keep from yelping in ecstasy.

"Oh, the big D can't handle it?" Threed said teasingly, though it sounded muffled as she hadn't taken my cock out of her mouth. Before I could answer, she started stroking it while moving her head up and down, the replica giggling and flicking her tongue across my balls.

"Shit, shit, I can't," I admitted. Maybe one day, but for now I pulled back, sighed, and grabbed Three by the ass before hefting her up and onto a ridge nearby.

The waterfall drowned out noise, and the walls were thick enough, and we were mid-flight, so I doubted whether the other girls would hear. Not that they'd care. I needed to rest but couldn't think about that at the moment. Right then, I needed to bring it like it had never been brought. So I squeezed her ass while she took my cock and guided it into her wet pussy.

It was tight, warm… home. Where I belonged. I slid in while bringing my lips to hers, pressing firmly and tasting her tongue, then moved my mouth to her neck while my hand that wasn't on her ass found her breasts. We were moving, faster, faster… Another set of hands found my back, moving down to my ass and I jumped, startled, as a finger attempted to work its way down there.

"No, no," I said, not ready for that yet. Someday, maybe? If I was drunk? A glance back showed me that Replica was pouting.

"You want me to get rid of her?" Threed asked. "Or maybe she wants company?"

I rolled my eyes, uncomfortable with what I assumed she wanted to do, but I said, "Fine."

She grinned, blinked again as she wrapped her legs around me and pulled my hips toward her to get the rhythm started again.

"This is weird," I heard myself say, but it wasn't me—it was my replica, standing behind me with her replica, his cock (well, my cock) fully erect and more impressive than I'd ever realized when glancing down at myself.

"Did you…?" I asked, losing focus.

"Dear, honey, sugar," she stared at me, frustrated. "I can only make exact copies. You really *are* that big."

I glanced back, smiled, and said, "Damn."

"Stop looking at my cock, er, me," my replica said, and then we both laughed, and I turned back to focus on Threed. A second later, moans and yelps of satisfaction sounded from the other two, so I knew they were going at it. Threed was watching over my shoulder as I pushed up into her, our two bodies becoming one.

As tingles spread through my body, sweat formed on my chest, and I lost any awareness of what was going on around me. I didn't give a shit if watching a very exaggerated version of a mirror of us turned her on.

Hell, it would probably turn me on too, if I could focus on anything at the moment aside from the amazing feeling of her tight pussy. My mind only had two thoughts running through it—damn, this felt good was the first. The second was the realization that this was only the beginning.

I was in for the weirdest, most amazing sex I'd ever had.

16

M y energy was surging when we landed outside the ruins, so much so that I was the first out, eyes searching for someone to hit. Navani had her chat with Threed, but by that point, Threed was so satisfied that she was acting like a completely different person. Maybe that's all it took to keep her from going into crazy zone—a good lay from time to time. Well, I'd do my part for the team.

"There," Navani said, eyes on the far hill. "His ships are lined up, ready to blow us to shit if we're stupid enough to go that way."

"And since he knows about your power," Sacrada pointed out, "he's likely set up a trap that way, figuring we'd avoid the first." She indicated an opening in the hills nearby.

Navani scanned the surrounding area, frowning. "Sacrada, you have some sort of sonar sensor?"

"Not exactly, but… similar." Sacrada rose up in the air, hair blowing behind her as the gold returned and the circles of light emanated from her. When they returned, she frowned.

"You too?"

"What?" I asked, and Threed was glaring at them.

"They're blocking sensors," Navani explained. "It gives them away, but since they know that we already know they're here, it doesn't matter much to them that we know they're here. What it means is we have no way of knowing how many of them there are."

"We'll have to do it the Marine Corps way then," I said. "Run in there and blow everything up. Kill 'em all, let God sort 'em out."

"Except for the whole situation with my sister," Sacrada reminded us.

"On that note," Threed said, and then pointed up to the sky past the hills. A large image appeared there, Sakurai lashed to a post with gleaming ropes, with Goros standing over her, leering at us.

"About damn time," he said. "I was starting to

consider draining her and seeing how long it would take. Maybe when we're done here."

Sacrada took a step forward, but Navani held up a hand. "He knows we're here, doesn't mean he knows our position. Don't give him that."

"Thing is," Goros continued. "I'd like her to see you all die just as much as I'd like you to see her die. So let's make this fun. You have one hour to get to her, but you won't. You'll all lose in your silly attempt to save her, and then I'll bring you here, keep you alive just long enough to watch me bathe in your blood, in her blood... and especially in the blood of our new friend, the son of the great Apollo. Shall we, then." He smiled up at the screen, then shot Sakurai full of his green electricity. She screamed, flickered out, and reappeared right where she'd been, sweating with the pain. "To show you I mean business, I'll hit her with one of those every fifteen minutes. And her little power of resetting... I have it in check. This will be fun for all of us, I hope you agree."

He walked off screen, leaving the image of Sakurai there, groaning, fighting off the pain.

"When we get to him, he's mine," Sacrada growled, fists clenched and eyes glowing brighter than I'd seen before.

"No arguments here," I said.

"Why're we wasting time chatting about it?" Threed chimed in, already moving forward. "I'll scout." She split into three, her replicas breaking off left and right. "When they're done, I'll simply dismiss them—they vanish when I say so."

We followed the real Threed, moving for the tree line and then up the nearest hill. Halfway up, trees shifted to our left, and there was a shout that sounded like Threed. A piercing scream sounded, during which we saw in the distance a green-clad supervillain running along bent trees in pursuit of Threed's replica. It was no good though, as the trees moved in on her and vines caught her, dragging her down to the ground, choking her off, cutting into her limbs.

"Don't worry about her," Threed hissed, though she was clearly being affected by it. Her face was pale, her hands clenching and unclenching. We darted on, unnoticed by the nature-controlling supers.

Navani gasped, pulled out her blaster, and then thought better of it. She whispered, "Move quietly,." With a quick glance, she added, "Still have your hype?"

I moved my arms, feeling how responsive they

were, how pumped full of energy they felt from my romp with Threed and nodded.

"Good, but… in case you need a bit more." She grabbed me by the back of my head, pulled me in for a passionate kiss, and then said, "Go."

The extra boost helped, and I felt unstoppable as I charged through the dense foliage, moving forward while angling to the right. As she'd guessed, there was a super, crouched and waiting. He saw me a split second before my fist made impact, and I didn't stop. I'd learned my lesson about hesitating back when fighting those stupid alligator mutations. This time, I capitalized on my combo skills and came in with a series of rapid punches to his gut—mini-uppercuts— that I knew wouldn't do much to hurt him, but would charge up my attack. And when I grabbed him by the back of his head and pulled him in for a knee to the face, I almost felt sorry for the guy.

My knee made impact, his face splattered like mush, and I stepped back, gagging. That shit was disgusting.

"Try to be cleaner, next time," a voice said, and I looked up to see a super hanging like a spider. She wore a tight black one-piece with a red cloak hanging open, eight eyes across her face, and spiderwebs tangling from her arms. Hack all that nastiness off of her, and she could've been hot.

Was I cursed, that even supers who were about to try and kill me got the attractive or not assessment? Eh, whatever.

Her webs shot out, starting to surround me, instantly draining the energy I'd stored up. We hadn't much tested my abilities to turn powers back on their users yet, and in this case, it didn't work. Maybe it only worked when it was related to non-solid projectiles, like fire and lasers?

At any rate, my shields weren't doing a damn thing either. Probably because this wasn't a projectile. It seemed she'd found a way around my defenses. Luckily for me, I had friends and had no problem being saved in moments like this. With a whistle to indicate I had problems, hoping they'd catch on, I threw myself to the ground to avoid being in the line of attack when they came.

What I didn't count on was that they'd show up being pursued by several other supers who had, it seemed, found their location.

Sacrada threw an attack at the spider super, but she had a shield that blocked it. When more supers came from behind, Sacrada's attention was diverted. My head was starting to spin, my mouth going dry. Navani was shielding herself and shooting with her expert precision, while Threed had reunited with her replica and were doing their damage against a man that resembled a walking bull.

I had an idea.

"Attack me!" I shouted at Sacrada. She frowned at me, cut through an enemy with her wings, and then did as I asked.

A little too eagerly, if you ask me. Her blast of sunburst shot at me, and I thought I was going to die in an instant, even screamed as the pain of being burned alive took hold—but only for a second, and then it was gone like it had never happened. But I felt it in my hands, saw them light up with red and gold energy, and then grabbed the webbing that held me there.

An inside route through her shields. It worked as I'd hoped, the flames and energy shooting up through the arachnid's webbing, blasting her from the insides. The smoke came first, then her eyes melted—all eight of them—and then she fell from the tree as she burst into flames.

My flames died down, energy spent, and I tore the remaining strands of burnt webbing off. It had worked. I couldn't believe it had worked!

Something hit me, and I spun to attack, but it was a good thing I was too weakened from the spider web. It was Navani, and she hit me again.

"Don't ever fucking try that again, you hear me!" she shouted. "That was reckless, foolish—"

"Badass!" Threed shouted. "Totally makes me want to go down on him right now, right? You too?" She beamed, then charged past me and hit the bull-man in the throat as he'd been about to charge Navani. Green shot out from her fist and, as he tried to stand, still gasping for air, the green flew into him and he started writhing, screaming. At my look of curiosity, she said, "It's like a mixture of poison and acid. Does wonders for cleaning mildew in tight spots."

"Um, yes, sexy... very," Navani said to me, composing herself. "But still, not cool. You scared me half to death."

"Sorry," I said. "But it worked."

"Huh," Sacrada said, lowering herself to our side. Apparently, this little group of supers was out of the picture. "I wasn't sure myself."

"And yet you did it?" Navani said. "Do I have to remind you all that we're doomed without him and his seed?"

The rest of us cracked up at that, and I felt my energy returning to normal. "To be fair, there's still my brother," I pointed out. "Assuming he gets off of that prison ship."

They seemed to consider that, when Threed

came back, grabbed my package and licked my cheek. "Yup, tastes like sexy man."

I suppressed a chill of excitement that ran up my spine, moved her hand aside, and said, "We might want to move. I'm guessing all that noise gave away our position."

"Ah, just a quick blow job?" Threed said, pouting.

"No time," Navani interjected. "I think she's joking, but seriously, just in case… no time."

Threed grinned and shrugged as she split again, bringing back the final replica. "We'll never know, will we?"

They all three took off, going in different directions again. My hype was back somewhat from the energy rush of Threed grabbing me, and I had a feeling she knew exactly what she was doing there.

"You got this?" Navani asked, looking me over with worry.

"Actually," I replied as we ran, pulling up my screen, "I reached another level. One more to five! Then I get some sort of celebration, or what?"

"Just shut up and use the skill point before we face any more of them."

I went right away to the attack skill tree, selecting the first in a set of three—I did this one, even though it was only a simple chance of stunning my opponents' skill, because of the one it would unlock for the next skill point. On level five, I'd be able to get one that could crack through an opponent's shield, leaving them susceptible to projectile attacks.

As the upgrade went through, I nearly tripped on a root sticking up out of the ground and had to remind myself to watch where I was going. The screen went away, and I pulled out my blaster, wondering if I should also get some of the skills that related to shooting, soon. I'd always been a good shot, but that was with Marine Corps weapons. These blasters and whatnot were a different beast, and one of the skill branches had related to aim, thermal sight or night vision, and various other upgrades. It was weird thinking of myself as a super whose powers were mostly related to hand-to-hand combat and shooting, but hey, I wasn't the typical super.

What really boggled my mind was what we'd discovered about my powers. If I took the fact that I could get lasting energy from something like sex, and could somewhat absorb another super's powers by being targeted, what if I combined those two? Could I make the fire power I'd borrowed from Sacrada last longer, using it throughout?

That would have to wait though because we crested the hill and found ourselves at the edge of the maze of ruins, more hills and caverns, all leading through to the massive fortress at the center. Supers rose in the sky, preparing to bombard us with attacks as we worked our way through, and all I could think was that they were all dead meat.

17

W e charged through a nearby grouping
of trees just as a gust of wind
whipped up a barrage of rocks and
sticks and other debris at us. Two supers kept their
distance, a third sweeping up close and shooting
down a flurry of blades.

Navani threw her arm up and cast a shield, but
two of the blades made it through, landing an inch
from my foot.

"Watch it!" I shouted, leaping over them and
heading for the point where the trees were thickest.

"I got this," Sacrada said, as Threed ran up next to
me, nudging me with her elbow.

"Wanna see something cool?" she asked. "I
dismissed my replicas and... check it out."

My response was a crazy look as I kept running, but when I glanced back I saw her eyes light up, and she made two copies of Sacrada so that they split off and started raining fire and brimstone down upon our opponents.

Sacrada shot her sunburst at the enemy, then shouted down, "Don't ever fucking do that again without my permission!"

"She'll thank me when the enemy's dead and her sister is saved," Threed said, sprinting over to catch up with me. The look in her eyes wasn't as certain as her voice, though. Above, the flying supers were quite occupied trying to deal with the three Sacradas, so that the rest of us were able to reach cover and then descend into a bit of a valley that led along the ridge of a hillside cliff. We hadn't gone three steps when the rocks in front of us burst open, and a man forming into rocks appeared as the other supers flew overhead, giving him cover.

When he charged, I didn't know what the fuck to do. Sliding sideways, I shot him with my blaster, but it didn't do any good. Threed lunged forward to try tripping him, but her leg hit with a thud and it did no good. She cried out in pain as she held her injured leg while dancing about on the other.

Navani took the brunt of the attack, throwing up a purple shield that the rock-man slammed into, pushing her back. He rained down blow after blow until the shield shattered, forcing Navani to fall back with a grunt.

The rock-man lifted an arm to strike and I ran forward, figuring I had to do something. "Shoot me," I told Threed as I ran.

"What?"

"Just do it!" I replied, "I need my shield to break."

She caught my blaster, and I didn't linger to see if she understood. I leaped up slamming my fists into the rock-man. FUCK! That hurt. Each punch I gave him stung like hell, and by the fourth, I could feel an intense pain shooting up my arm. I heard something snap, but then with the fifth strike I caught him with my stun power.

He stumbled back, but it wasn't enough.

"Now!" I shouted to Threed, and she unleashed on me as I charged the rock-man again.

"What're you doing?!" Navani was up now, confused, but I held my hand up and shouted with rage. The fact that she was watching me, that I was defending her, it all processed in my mind and I felt a surge of the hype—it wasn't only sexualized, I remembered. If this act of bravery and sacrifice while she watched somehow impacted on my hormones, that would do the trick.

And that explained why, even though the rock-man hit me and sent me flying, I wasn't severely damaged when I popped back up.

Navani had opened up fire on the rock-man, but he was blocking the shots with his arms.

"Not at him. At me!" I shouted as I charged him again. I punched with my less injured arm and then watched as my shield flashed blue with a hit from Threed and shattered. In the process, a shock wave went out and hit the rock-man so that he was actually knocked back, stumbling, and fell.

"Blaster!" I shouted to Threed, and she tossed it to me. I caught it, stepped up to the bastard, and put it point blank against his eye. "Shield this, fucker."

With a sizzling Pssszzzt, he was gone.

Navani glided down, looking impressed. "Nice work."

"Damn, D," Threed said, nodding. "That was impressive."

"Agreed," Navani said but pointed at the image of Sakurai above. "Keep moving."

Nobody argued with that. We pushed on, but a roaring sound came from overhead. None of us wanted to check it out, so we just ran. Finally, Sacrada stopped, pulling Threed to a halt next to her. "Do it."

"What?"

"Dismiss the others and replicate me. Send the

replica up to scout it out. Do another, but of Navani to focus on shielding the replica. While we go one way, they can go the opposite of the enemy, giving us an idea of which way to go to reach Goros while also leading whatever group pursues off our tracks."

"Sounds too strategic for my tastes," Threed said with a shrug. "But if you say so."

Her eyes lit up, and she first made the replica of Sacrada, then Navani. If I wasn't so focused on the fight at that moment, I could've easily imagined one of the best orgies of my life.

They knew their mission and darted off, while we pushed on along the cliff face, watching to see what would happen.

"I can't imagine the crazy stuff in life you've done with your powers," I said to Threed once we'd slowed our pace, trying to focus on what was going on above. So far, it seemed Sacrada was circling, not seeing anything. That didn't seem right.

"Well, my first lover was obsessed with anal, and I hated the idea," she said. "So I'd send my replica in while I waited in the bathroom. He never had a clue."

"Didn't you feel it?" I asked. "I mean, do you?"

Sacrada grunted, clearly uncomfortable with the conversation.

"I feel a portion of whatever they feel. Like what you hear when someone speaks through a wall. So…

it felt good. Actually, after a while, I started to like the idea, and boy was he confused when we first tried and he couldn't get it in."

I laughed, but then shook my head. "It doesn't have to be sexual. I meant, like... I don't know. Having them do chores is too boring, but didn't you ever do something like that?"

"All the time. Just, around you, I'm having a hard time thinking of anything non-sexual."

"Stop," Navani said, glancing up. "Too much."

"Just because you don't have the appetite I do," Threed said. "Remember, I gotta feed the beast for three ladies at once."

"My sexual appetite is just fine, especially when it comes to Drew here," Navani said. "But look..."

We glanced up and froze. Or maybe froze was a weird word choice, because the duplicate of Sacrada had frozen too. And then she started to fall.

"No," the real Sacrada said, stepping out and wings spreading.

"It's not really you," Navani warned. "Let her go."

A super flew through the air with gusts of billowing gray and white clouds following her, a flurry of snow gushing out and then spears of ice pierced the replica. As we watched, the super homed in on something below, and then swept down on it like a hawk.

"Impossible," Sacrada said, glaring at her. "No ice super could stand a chance against me."

"Well, that statement was just proven wrong," Threed said, and suddenly Sacrada grimaced with pain as her replica met her final moment.

"One thing we know. We don't want to face her," Navani said emphatically, and we took off again, faster now. Not even three paces later Navani cringed, her replica gone too. We kept on, pushing around the hill and then climbing over a section that we felt sure would take us on a faster route to the center.

A small metallic item leaped into the air, flashing and screeching, clearly giving away our location. And then the source of the rumbling arrived. The sky was crackling and breaking apart as three supers, dark as the night, flew in. It was like the day was giving way to darkness from another dimension.

"The Nihilists," Sacrada said, voice breaking in fear. "Get to cover, now."

We turned back the way we'd come, Sacrada's fear of them pushing her into the lead. There was no time to ask for an explanation, but I knew they had to be bad. Going off her level of fear alone, I figured they were more badass than Goros, and probably only a step or two below this Ranger fellow.

The ground split behind us, a large chunk of it suddenly vanishing, and then the air nearby was replaced by nothingness—it was hard to explain, except that there was the sudden knowledge of it simply being nothingness.

"Don't let them into your head," Navani shouted, pushing herself to catch up with Sacrada and pointing us toward a series of caves not far off.

"How do we do that?" I asked.

"Focus on something else, anything else."

My eyes went to her ass, and I grinned. "Easy."

She glanced back and laughed. "That'll do. Who here has Drew's hard cock in their mind right now?"

"Ladies," Sacrada said, glancing back with fear.

"Not me, I'm imagining his soft balls," Threed said. "Sucking on them like little eggs. Mmm."

"What the fuck?" I said.

"Hey, you started it," Navani reminded me.

"But you're all ganging up on me," I replied, about to say more when Sacrada shrieked, and then lost consciousness mid-stride. She fell forward, slamming her face into the rocky ground, and then just kept sliding another yard or two. When I reached her, I slung her up over my shoulder while Threed and her replica stuck close, ready for more action.

We all kept moving, but slower now, and

suddenly Sacrada's eyes flashed open, black, and she struck out at both of us. Threed leaped out of the way, though her replica took the brunt of that attack. It hurt me, but mostly I absorbed the attack although I had to let her go, lest my flaming hands do damage to her. I wasn't sure whether or not that could happen but thought probably not. I just didn't know if supers were typically immune to their own powers.

"They have her," Threed said, running off without another glance back.

"We need distance," Navani shouted, then turned and glanced over her shoulder at the slope behind is. It led down to a river, and I was already dreading where this was going.

"No, you can't be—" I was going to say serious, but she had already grabbed hold of Sacrada and me, throwing herself over so that we all went with her.

"Threed!" she shouted as we fell, and I lost all concept of what was happening. We were rolling, hitting rocks, getting tossed about. Screaming, grunting. A sharp pain hit my back, and then I went flying into the air to land with a heavy thump.

A groan sounded to my right, and there was Sacrada pushing herself up, eyes back to their normal golden state.

"Wha—what happened?" she asked.

"They got to you and—duck!" Navani shouted.

Sacrada reacted in time, lowering her head as Threed hit a rock and went flying over her, to land in the river. She jumped up in a flash, holding her shoulder and grunting.

"Keep moving!" Navani said. "They're going to follow." She glanced around, eyes landing on a nearby cave. "That one."

We all agreed and ran for it.

18

We entered the cave and kept running, moving along a passage to the right and looping around until it came to a narrow opening. From there we were able to peer out, see that the skies in this direction were empty, and debate our next move.

"There are too many of them!" Sacrada said, hugging herself and glancing over at Threed, who stood there shivering. "Goros has too many supers, and they're too powerful!"

"No, I don't think that's true," I said, stepping forward. We were left with one option here, and that was to test my theory. I explained it to them, about how I could retain my powers longer and stronger after sex, and how maybe I could store their powers too. If this worked, we'd have a distinct advantage—all of us, plus me with their powers.

"Let me get this straight," Sacrada said, her eyebrow raised. "You want us, in the middle of this battle... when we could be attacked at any minute... to all fuck you."

"Not only fuck him," Threed said with a laugh, "but fuck him while hitting him with our powers. Giving him everything we've got. Kinky as hell, so you know I'm in."

"I could put up shields, so at least they couldn't enter without giving us a warning," Navani said. "I've sworn my life to this mission and will try anything to ensure victory. It sounds dangerous... and fun."

"So I'm the only one of us who thinks this is stupid as hell?" Sacrada asked.

"You saw the way your powers worked on him," Navani reminded her. "And there's no doubt about how his body reacts to hormonal changes. We have to try it."

Sacrada looked at me, her eyes moving back and forth across mine, her chest heaving. For a brief moment, she seemed to be considering it, then turned and shouted, "I'm not having a fucking orgy while my sister's out there being tortured! Possibly killed!"

"You don't have to," I pointed out. "You have rage, you're pissed... I need your powers most of all here."

"What?" Her nostrils were flared, her chest now rising and falling rapidly, but she was listening.

"You're frustrated, right? Well, we've seen that when you hit me with your powers, I can use them. I think if it's related to all this other hormonal stuff, I can store them. So... we'll do our best to make this quick, while you unleash your frustration in a different way—by blasting me to hell. It'll hurt like hell if it's anything like what I've seen. But it won't actually burn me or have lasting effects."

"Only, we hope he doesn't die, and it all actually works out in our favor," Navani said.

Threed traced my neckline, nibbling at my earlobe. "I'm going to like this."

"Too much, I imagine," I said, squeezing her ass and making her yelp, more to piss off Sacrada than anything else.

It worked because her eyes flared and she nodded. At that, Navani turned and threw up a couple shields.

"How do we—" I started to ask, suddenly realizing how awkward the situation was, but I should've known that Threed had it covered. She already had two replicas tearing off my clothes as she undressed, then they threw me back while she stood over me, watching, starting to touch herself and massage her breasts. Navani was slightly taken aback, but I reached for her, pleading. She shook her head with a look of uncertainty, and then pulled off her outfit. Damn, there was something sexy about the way she hesitated.

"Get in here," one of the replicas said, standing and taking her by the hand, guiding her over to me. Holding her hand, the replica placed it on my leg, pulling it up to caress my balls, and then working my cock together. It was now as firm as it could get, and the real Threed moved in for my mouth, then knelt over me, facing my cock as if she were going to do a sixty-nine.

"Lick it," she commanded me, and her pussy was in my face. At this point, I didn't give a shit about all of the stupid stuff she'd done up to this point—her sexy pussy was calling me, so I kissed her thighs, started licking and loving it. There were at least two mouths on my cock, hands on my balls and one starting to tickle my ass. I still wasn't sure about that part, but right then I didn't care.

I glanced down to see Navani taking charge, into it now and moving the two replicas aside so she could straddle me.

"That's okay," Threed said between her ecstatic moans, "I've always preferred leftovers."

Navani rolled her eyes, then slid her pussy around my cock. My back arched and I nearly bit down on Threed, it felt so good. My slight nibble made her squeal, and she asked for more. She was kinky, moving back and sticking her breasts in my face, rubbing them back and forth and even hitting me with them a couple of times as she laughed.

"Do it," she said to Sacrada. "Make him squirm now."

A look of worry came over Navani, but she started riding me harder, working me up to the point of near climax, while Threed moved around to her back and reached down, grabbing hold of my balls and rubbing a hand over Navani's clit.

"Shh, he likes to watch," Threed said, and Navani didn't fight it. She was right, that sight was to die for. The replicas moved on to kissing my neck and chest, my hands groping them, and then Sacrada was suddenly bright and floating over us as her first attack came.

It was aimed at my face, to avoid hitting Navani or Threed, but she didn't mind hitting the replicas.

As fire and pain took hold of me, I squeezed one of the replica's tits so hard I was surprised it didn't pop. She screamed and laughed, while the other moaned in my ear, sticking her fingers in my mouth for me to bite down on. I had to wonder if they were even kinkier than Threed, somehow, or if they were exactly like her. The thought was fleeting as more pain hit me along with the pleasure. There was the external heat and burning, then the internal running up my legs, filling my chest, and I wanted to scream for it to stop, but instead bit down on those fingers and pushed through it.

One of the replicas took my fingers and jammed them inside of her, screaming and loving it as she burst into flames, and I had to close my eyes to keep from being totally turned off by how insane they were getting.

Suddenly they were gone, both replicas, and Threed was yelping, having shoved Navani off of me and now slamming herself down on my cock. The flames stopped for a second while Threed came and tore into me with her fingernails, sending green light that drifted down and burned in a more stinging way than the flames, and when she was done she rolled off, and Navani took her turn again, this time pulling me over to be on top.

I took control, feeling the surge of energy, the pain gone everywhere except for from Threed's fingernails, and I glanced up to see a hunger in Sacrada's eyes. She licked her lips, staring at me passionately, and I stared back as her hand moved across her breast, exposing it, while she took a step toward me.

Her eyes moved up to the direction where the sky was over our roof, where she knew that image of her sister was, and paused.

"More?" she asked.

"Do it," I said, and as I felt Navani's pussy clench and get wet, I knew I was about to come too. My balls slapped against her ass as my hands gripped her hips, and the blast hit me again.

This time, I was on the point of orgasm, and the pain and pleasure tore through me at the same time, my cock surging larger than I was sure it had ever been before. Navani yelped, eyes wide as she screamed, "Oh my gods!" and came again, and I was still orgasming, still feeling the pain of the solar burst, and then it was done, and we were done, panting, my cock still in her, Threed lying there laughing hysterically.

"Oh my gods, oh my gods," Threed repeated, mockingly.

"Shut up," Navani said between deep breaths, eyes closed, lost in the moment. "I've never…"

"Tell me about it," Threed said, coming back over and slapping me on the ass, then mimicking as if she was doing me. "I don't think I've ever had so much fun."

Sacrada however, had a conflicted look of pain and frustration. "Stop messing around and get dressed. We have to capitalize on the moment."

"She's right," Navani said, eyes popping open. She started to stand but fell back. "She's... Oh, shit. Holy... shit. Your cock was so huge. I mean, it's always good, but right now? Damn."

"I felt it too," I said with a smile, leaning in and kissing her.

"Okay, now it's getting weird," Threed said, already up and dressing. "We came, we burned, we conquered. Well, three of us came, all of us are about to conquer. But you get the idea. Get the fuck up people, we have some bad guys to mutilate!"

For the first time ever that I'd seen, Sacrada gave the woman a look that wasn't a frown. "Yes, Threed. Thank you."

"Hey, the sooner we rescue your sis, the sooner you might get that stick out of your butt and fuck our boy here," Threed said with a wink. "I'm just thinking of the mission, that's all. And I wouldn't mind seeing that prude face of yours all scrunched up with your O-face."

"Right," Sacrada said. "I'll... be outside. Hurry."

I helped Navani up, though she had to use some leaves to catch the extra cum that spilled out, as there'd been a damn lot. If this hadn't impregnated her, I kind of wondered if it would ever happen. But I wasn't about to say that. Not here, not now.

We quickly dressed, and I felt like I could take on the world. Hell, as we took down the shields and exited the cave, I felt like I was the world. Nothing could stop me. Good thing, too, because there was Goros on the screen again, reminding us that we'd used up half of our time as he shocked Sakurai again. That fueled my rage, and as we left the cave and started to run toward his fortress, I felt the flames surging from my hands, the green energy seeping out around me, and even a bit of purple—like Navani—glowing as my eyes took on a different hue. It was unlike anything I'd ever experienced before. Suddenly I could see images of people, moving about within that castle. Supers, preparing for the defense. It was like thermal sights but on crack.

My screen was even popping up, reading their powers to me. One there with the ability to move matter, one with shields, one that could read minds and was now likely telling Goros we were approaching, fast.

Good. Let him know we were coming. I couldn't wait to get my hands on him.

19

The thing was, we were ready to go but still had too much ground to cover. Damn. I started thinking about huge-ass eagles carrying us or something, wondering what our options were, when I glanced over at Threed. She winked at me—a habit of hers that she did too often —and I realized how easy it was.

"We're going to need copies of Sacrada again," I said.

"Hey, if she's not putting out, her copies won't either," Threed replied.

Sacrada grunted. "What for?"

"Think you can carry someone?" I asked. "I mean, you're damn powerful, but will the wings support it."

"Of course," she replied, and then her eyes went to me, Navani, and Threed. "Oh, of course!"

Threed caught on now, as did Navani, and soon we were standing each with our own Sacrada, ready to take to the skies.

"You freak out up there, I might drop you," Sacrada warned. "Just… don't freak out. Stay calm in my arms. You're going to have to be the weapon because I can't use my powers without the use of my hands."

"Roger that," I replied, and the others agreed they would be good.

"Okay. Loverboy, you're with me," she glared. "I don't want you getting all gropy with a replica and me not knowing about it. At least this way, you do that, I let you fall."

"I'm not some perv trying to grope a feel," I pointed out. "Nothing here has been without full consent and, in fact, Navani's the one who propositioned me."

"Right, well… my point remains."

"Let's get on with it, while Drew still has our powers," Navani suggested. "And before we're all slaughtered."

The others agreed, so the three Sacradas grabbed hold of us from behind, under the arms, and took off, shooting into the air. She was strong, I could feel that, but worried she wouldn't be able to hold us up there like that forever.

Other supers flew out to meet us, but the Sacradas did a great job of dodging, and whatever they couldn't dodge, Navani was able to throw up shields against. Her Sacrada kept to the back so that they could get a good view, with Threed in the middle to stay guarded. If she got hurt or even distracted, her attention would falter, and the replicas would go bye-bye.

Which meant I was on point. With the fire powers of Sacrada, I was quite all right with that. I threw out blasts of fire as if I'd been born to do just that. When a super tried to hit me with a series of blades, I burned off his ugly face. Another came at us with wings one minute, no wings the next, thanks to yours truly.

And then that damn super with the clouds and the ice was approaching.

"We need to get there faster!" Navani shouted.

"Get us the damn spaceship and maybe we would be," Sacrada shouted back.

"Except, then we would've broken the stupid rules of this game," I pointed out, though I wasn't sure if they heard me. The point had been that he could kill Sakurai whenever he wanted to but was using her as leverage so that we'd play along. I had to wonder, if we got too close, would he just kill her anyway.

Another idea struck me. Damn, I was on a roll.

"Throw me at her," I said, indicating the crazy storm super.

"What?" Sacrada asked. "All that sexing made you lose your mind?"

"Not if I can steal her powers," I said. "If she thinks I'm coming in for an attack, she'll blast me. Then… you get the idea."

"And what if, one day, you get hit by powers that you can't absorb, and they leave you dead?"

"I'm going to bet on that never happening," I replied. "Because if it does, I'm dead anyway so I won't care. In the meantime, I can be a superhero."

"In the meantime, you can be a crazy son of a bitch," she said but swooped up while yelling for the others to continue with the plan. The storm super came for us, following Sacrada's lead, and then Sacrada spun, wings gleaming in the sunlight, and tossed me.

It's a strange feeling, knowing you can't fly and being tossed through the air at a murderous supervillain.

But I started blasting with my fire, threw up a couple shields to protect against her ice spears, and then her blast of freezing air came at me. This is what I was waiting for—no shields, no solar bursts to try and counteract it. I spread my limbs and took it like a man.

DAMN, it was cold. Like dipping your balls into a bucket of ice-cold water, only that horrible feeling of your balls leaping up into your stomach was all over, and I wanted to piss myself just for the memory of what it felt like to be warm.

It lasted a second, and then it was gone.

In its place, was a sensation like I'd just chewed the strongest winterfresh gum ever, coursing through my limbs. When I threw it back at her, I found out that, no, not all supers are immune to their own powers. She froze and then started to fall.

Meanwhile, clouds had formed around me, winds gusting and whistling, and I pushed myself on after Sacrada, who was whooping in a very uncharacteristic way, shouting about how awesome it was, what I'd just done.

If there was ever a panty dropping move for her, it seemed I'd just done it.

So we converged on the fortress, Sacrada throwing fire and chaos, me with my newfound ability to barrage them with ice spears and freezing gusts of wind. The first group of supers didn't stand a chance, and when I saw Sakurai on the pedestal,

Goros turning to make eye contact with me, I knew he had no intention of letting her live.

That's why, with no thought my own safety and ignoring the fact that I could lose these powers at any moment, as soon as the effect of my sex-party boost wore off, I dove straight for him throwing a barrage of everything I had. Fire, ice, wind, storm clouds, and when he lifted his hands to end Sakurai, I was already there, slamming my fist into his arm with a green explosion of acid gas that left him stumbling back, coughing and growling in pain.

Ice spears surrounded him, some were broken apart by his lightning, but he was shivering, and I could tell I'd had an impact. He looked around, realizing we'd made it farther than he ever thought possible and that he'd suffered from hubris to the point that he had no guards.

It was him and me.

So he ran.

"Coward!" I shouted but hesitated. Sacrada flew up behind me and said, "Go, I'll rescue my sister."

With a nod of thanks, I flew after the motherfucker. He was charging down passages, filling his surroundings with that green lighting that sent walls and ceilings crumbling down on me, but my power from Navani still allowed me to throw up shields, so I was safe. At a hole in the floor, he leaped down, hit a passage two down, and rolled out of sight. I followed, throwing a blast of ice. An *oomph* sounded from below, and I imagined he'd slipped and fell, but by the time I was there, he had vanished.

The sounds of fighting nearby told me the others were still at it, but our victory here wouldn't be as sweet if we didn't catch Goros.

It was only when I attempted to fly another time that I realized my powers were fading. It wasn't that I couldn't fly, yet, but that it was more of a gentle shove than the catapult of power it had been moments before.

And then he was there, leering at me, and he struck—only, it wasn't just him. Three supers appeared at his side, the Nihilists. At that moment all I could do was panic, and I felt my mind going black. One of the Nihilists threw out black shadows and hit me, and it was like I was somewhere else entirely. For that moment I was in a strange world, only it was the same one, and those Nihilists were tall, alien forms without robes or any blackness. We were in their world, and instead of controlling me, I had absorbed their power, gone over to their dimension.

They were looking at me nervously, realizing that I shouldn't be there, confused. For my part, I wasn't going to sit around doing nothing. It was take the hill or die trying for me. Can't shoot it, how's the saying go? Shoot it some more, or something like that.

So I tried powers. Nothing. I tried my blaster—it wasn't there… I was nude! Apparently Lamb, or her essence-enhanced biotech suit, couldn't travel over to their dimension with me. Oh, well, I'd do this the old-fashioned way. Fight naked, like the gods of Ancient Greece. See, I studied military history, so I knew that much. Or at least, how the paintings liked to portray them.

Charging forward, dick swaying in the wind, I pulled back my fist, then let it fly.

BAM! The first of these creatures took it right in the face, his head spinning and his spine cracking. At least I was still me and could hit like a man. The other two pulled back in horror, totally confused about what was happening, and when I grabbed the next one and head-butted him, his head caved in, leaving him an instant corpse.

The third gave me one look and vanished.

Like that, I was back in my clothes, back in our dimension, staring at Goros. He looked back at me with wide eyes, a trembling lower lip.

"You… how…?" he asked. "Impossible!"

"Tell me who they are," I demanded. "Or what."

"There's no way you saw them in their true form. I… I don't understand."

I stepped toward him, noticing a green spark come from my hand. It seemed I'd been hit by him during that encounter, and still had some of his power left.

"Last chance," I said, grabbing hold of him and pulling back my fist. When he saw the sparks, he muttered something about giving his life for the cause and drew a blade from his belt. That, I couldn't absorb. I could be impaled by it, yes, but no to absorbing its energy for my own benefit.

So I blasted him. Energy pulled from all around me, coursing through him, sending him flying back and against the wall. It continued to stream at him, slamming him over and over, but he shot back too, refusing to die so easily. Lines of green electricity were darting off, hitting walls, ceiling, and floor. With a thrust of my hands, I pulled harder, and the blast exploded, walls falling in, and the whole place caved in around us.

For a moment, I was pulled back into the other dimension, if that's what it was, and there was Lamb, staring at me in confusion.

"You discovered it," she said in awe. "None of us were able, but you… discovered it."

"I'm not following," I said. A glance down showed I was floating, nude again, and she was actually there, in the flesh.

"I crossed over," she said. "It was part of the sacrifice, but not the others. We didn't know I'd end up here, all we know is that the invaders, Ranger and his forces—this is where they get their real energy. And they have a fleet, too, whoever these creatures are. We were unable to harm them in our dimension, but here… maybe."

"Where are you?" I asked.

Her eyes roamed over me, and she smiled. "You'll do well, on your mission. And when it's over, maybe you can come find me?"

She started to fade, or so I thought at first, but then realized I was fading. "Lamb! Where?"

"I don't know," she admitted. "But I spotted you the first time, was able to pull you back… but I think it's used the last of my reserves. At the ship, hurry. I might be gone before you return, stuck here forever unless you can find me."

"How?" I shouted. "How?!"

But no answer came.

I wasn't there anymore, but thrust through the air, flying. No, falling! I was above the collapsed fortress, the jagged, broken rocks threatening to kill me when I landed. Sacrada swooped in, snatching me up, and she held me tight, not from behind, but in an embrace. We spun in the air, her wings flapping, and then she tilted her head, looked at me with those big, golden eyes, and said, "Thank you."

With that, she kissed me. Her lips were like honey if it were alive, like melted brown sugar. Every moment with my lips pressed against hers was a lifetime of bliss so that when she pulled her lips away, I felt lost without them.

"My sister is safe," she said. "I owe that to you."

"And... Goros?" I asked, turning to look down at the fallen fortress.

"Navani was scanning and hasn't seen any sign of him. You were gone too, for a few minutes. I was looking for you, I couldn't accept it. And then suddenly you were there, falling from the sky." She gave me a curious look. "Care to tell me about it?"

"Maybe later," I said. "I'm still trying to understand it myself."

She nodded, then flew us to the ground where Navani, Threed, and Sakurai waited.

We had just landed, when Goros pushed his way out of the fallen stones, glaring at me, screaming. "I know, master. It won't happen. He won't destroy everything we've built. You can count on me..."

He came at me, that knife still clutched in his hand. The others moved to interfere, but I held up a hand.

"No, I'm taking care of this asshole my way. The Marine Corps way."

He came at me with the knife in a straight thrust, and my old MCMAP training kicked in. I stepped into it, hitting the inside of his wrist with one hand and the outside with the other so that the blade went flying. Next, I wrapped his arm up and around, putting him in an armbar.

"Surrender," I said.

"Go eat shit," he spat out, pulling his own arm out of its socket as he swung at me with his other hand.

This time I simply stepped back and gave him a roundhouse kick to the face, and as he was already bent over, I barely had to lift my leg past hip level to do so. It sent him sprawling onto his back, and before he could get up I had him in a chokehold, using his cloak like a *gi* to choke one side of his neck, my knuckles pressed against the other.

"For the last time," I said, but he was already trying to strike me, so I leaned in and applied pressure, not letting go until he stopped flailing about.

"Is he... dead?" Navani asked.

"Unconscious, but he'll have a hell of a headache when he wakes," I said. "We're going to want to take him prisoner and get whatever intel we can. He knows something, related to the ones you called the Nihilists.

They all looked at me with confusion, all but Nivani. She had a knowing look in her eyes and nodded.

"We have a holding cell," she said. "It can at least last until we find an allied post to leave him in a brig somewhere. He'll talk, or he'll rot. Well, either way, he'll probably rot."

"Good," I said, and then walked over to Sakurai. "We never had a chance to really get to know each other. I'm Drew."

She looked at me with dazed eyes and then fainted. Sacrada caught her, holding her close.

"She needs rest," Sacrada said. "Let's get her to the ship."

"Lamb," Navani said. Nothing happened. "Lamb, please bring the ship."

Again, no response. My mind flashed back to the image of Lamb in the other dimension, and what she'd said.

"Lamb might not be able to respond," I said, really not wanting to explain how I knew this.

"I'm... still here..." A faint voice said, and then the ship arrived, flying low. "Hurry."

We all shared a look of confusion, then did our best to quickly board the ship.

Once we were on board, we made our way to the deck, and I called, "Lamb?"

Her voice replied, though her image didn't show. "I'm too weak," she said. "It's time... My essence will remain, in a sense. You will have the A.I. for the ship, the best A.I. out there, and you can refer to her as Lamb. In a way, it is sort of me. Likewise the suits. They'll still work as they have. But... it's my time."

"You never answered my question," I said.

Everyone looked at me with confusion.

"The Citadel," Lamb said. "The only answer I have is that, somehow, the power of the citadel might be the answer."

Navani nodded and told the others we'd explain when the time was right.

"I have good news, though," Lamb said. "Check the images, you'll see. For now... farewell."

"Goodbye, Lamb," I said, and the others gave their farewells, also.

Navani stepped up to the control panel and pulled up the images. There was my brother, holding hands with some women and jumping into what looked like a black hole. Only, there seemed to be people there, a city even. There was another image, one of the ship exploding, and another... of a woman in blue, staring out from a window. In the window, I could see the reflection of the exploding spaceship.

"A shuttle," Navani said. "She made it. Our sister."

"And my brother?" I asked.

"Quite possibly in the same place we'll find Lamb," Navani said, putting a hand on my shoulder. "It's all guesswork from here, but… we'll find him. And her. We'll make this right."

I put my hand on hers and looked around at the women with me. Strong, powerful, damn fine women. I couldn't ask for a better team.

20

Once the initial shock of the battle passed, and as we flew away from that planet to begin the next stage of our journey, we gathered in the mess hall. The ship sailed through space as we discussed the adventure, took a moment of silence for Lamb and the other Elders, and then ate a celebratory feast for the victory over Goros.

He hadn't given us anything to go on regarding the Nihilists and the other dimension yet, but Navani assured me she had her ways. I was famished and stuffed food into my face. Everyone appeared to be enjoying themselves, but Navani seemed lost in the stars.

"Ranger is still out there," she said, noticing my questioning look.

I nodded in understanding. "That, and now we know there's more to him than we thought."

"Even the Elders who sacrificed themselves, Xin and the others... they didn't know about this other realm or dimension. Whatever's going on here, I'd say it's going to blow our minds."

"Hey, I'm up for the adventure if you are," I leaned over and took her hand.

Threed had apparently heard the last part of the conversation, because she lifted her glass and said, "To the next part of our adventure!"

The other three smiled and raised their glasses. After the drink, I realized I'd had enough, so excused myself to shower and head back to the room I'd be using. No, nobody followed me into the shower, and I was glad for it. My super soldier was swollen, having done his job for this mission and then some. A little rest couldn't hurt, and then I'd wake up, ready to do whatever needed doing. Or whomever.

As I dried, I brought up my levels and skill points, grinned sleepily at the new skill point, and added the shield-piercer attack. It didn't matter now... but I was sure it would come in handy in the near future. That taken care of, I wandered back to my room as my mind raced with all of the memories of that battle. It had been glorious. One I could be proud of.

My room wasn't big—just a bed and a curved wall that went over my head, and it reminded me of sleeping in a closet under the stairs. Not something I'd done much of, but a distant memory recalled something like this from my youth when I'd still been moving around in foster homes. Those days were long gone. Among these strange people, these supers, I'd found my home at last.

The pillow was firm enough to give me support like I preferred, and I was just starting to close my eyes when the door slid open. Sakurai and Sacrada entered, eyeing me with curiosity. I sat up, trying to not be rude, but my head was already dozy and my attention unfocused.

"Hey," I said.

"My sister never had a chance to properly thank you," Sacrada said. "But just to be clear, I don't mean with sex. This whole thing, it's been too weird."

"I actually wanted to, but she talked me out of it," Sakurai said with a shrug. "So instead... Thank you." She laughed. "What do you think? Did that feel better than some good ol' fucking?"

I grinned. "Believe me, as much as I'd love to get with both of you, or either of you, whatever, I've had enough sex lately to last me until I die. Or at least until tomorrow."

"We're not ruling it out," Sacrada said, her tongue

subconsciously moving along her upper lip as she seemed to be lost in thought for a moment. "Just not using it as a way of saying thanks."

"Oh?" She had my attention.

"We're coming on the mission, we'll fight off whatever Ranger sends our way," Sacrada said. "And if along the way either of us decides we'd like to sleep with you, we will."

"Assuming I'll have you," I replied with a grin.

"Yeah, okay," Sacrada chuckled as she turned and left.

Sakurai lingered, a finger going to the edge of her mouth so she could bite it. "You know, I really want to. But she'd be so mad at me. Rain check?"

"I accept your raincheck for sex," I said. "As weird as that is."

"Okay." She gave me a wide grin and then spun on her heel in a way that caused her skirt to fly out and give me a nice view of her ass and her bright pink panties. Now I was starting to regret not trying to seduce her, but even at that thought my cock moved, rubbing against my pants. It hurt. A gentle reminder that it had been *way* overused lately.

At the moment, I only wanted to use it to take a piss. Then I was pretty sure I'd take a nice, long nap. As far as I knew, I'd been awake for way too long, and that hype energy could only keep me going so long.

"Lamb," I said, forgetting she wasn't there anymore. When no response came, it hit me, and I smiled, hoping she was in a better place. Still, I finished my thought. "Good night."

With that, I stumbled to the bathroom, let it out, and then hit the lights before falling into bed and letting sleep take me.

My dreams were of Earth, of an evening long ago when I'd met up with Chad and our adoptive parents, and been pleasantly enjoying each other's company, chatting and laughing. Nothing special about it, just a normal, pleasant evening. How foreign that concept seemed now.

At some point in the night, a finger pressed to my lips, waking me, and Navani's glowing blue eyes were there, not far from mine.

"I wanted you… all to myself," she said, and in my sleepy, dazed state she rode me. It was simple, it was pleasant. It was as it should be when two people feel that special connection. Somehow, this woman could still experience such an act with me regardless of everything and everyone else.

When it was over, she came first, then me, and I felt the grogginess fading, just as hers seemed to be starting to arrive.

I pressed my head onto her breasts, aware that they were damp but not sure if it was from my sweat or hers. With a long moan, I turned onto my back and lay there, panting, staring up at the curved ceiling.

Her hand found my still mostly hard cock and held it, tenderly. Even that soft touch sent an aftershock through my body.

"Trying to get me ready for round two?" I asked.

She leaned up on her elbow, hand moving to my balls and caressing them as if they were the most tender silk. "There'd be no need. There hadn't really been for this one, but I wanted to."

My eyes went wide. The smile that spread across her face was answer enough, but she said, "I knew it before, at the ruins. There was no doubt, the way you were pulsing in me, so huge, so…" A chill went down her spine, and she shivered. "If that didn't get me pregnant… Well, according to the ship's scanner, chances are very high. We don't know for sure yet, but will soon."

"So… we did it? We actually did it." I lay back and closed my eyes, but a worry washed over me. "I—I'm going to miss you."

"What?"

"I mean," I opened my eyes to see if I could read her expression. "Unless you're coming too? I just figured, since you basically have to go back to the Citadel and raise the child, teach him the ways."

She laughed. More of a giggle. "Oh, Drew… you silly Earther. Wait, you don't know?"

I sat up now, my mouth going dry at the look of worry in her eyes. "Know what?"

"Fuck. I thought I told you. Remind me to bitch slap someone for this. Okay, here's the thing. Now that I might be pregnant, which I'm going to bet is the case, it's just about to get interesting."

"Morning sickness?"

She laughed. "We all wish. No, now it's like there's a tracker in me. All of the bad guys who want to see to it that Earth was never created will be after me. Us."

"I'm not leaving your side," I said in realization, "because I'm going to stay and help defend you."

She beamed, nodding. "Because you're going to stay and help defend me."

Licking my lips as I processed this, I stood. Glancing back at her nude form lying there on her side, her perky breasts, I took a deep breath.

"No need to salute me," she said with a smile as my cock rose to full mast again. "A simple 'yes' will suffice."

Smiling, I crawled back into bed and straddled her, then said, "Yes," before moving in for round two.

No reason not to be safe, and after all, with everything coming our way, I wasn't sure how much longer I would be alive.

So yeah, I'd get seconds no matter how exhausted I was. I'd fight for her, and not just because she held the fate of her galaxy and mine in her womb.

She was kind. She was hot as hell. And she was mine. Hell, I might die, but oh well.

She was so fucking worth it. They all were.

THE END

AUTHOR RAMBLINGS

Book 1 in the Ex Gods series is done! How exciting. In case you weren't aware, this isn't exactly a book 2 from my SUPERS: EX HEROES series, but is in the Supers universe. That means I'm planning an Ex Heroes 2, which will be next, then Ex Gods 2. I hope you've had time to read them all before the next books come out! Ex Heroes follows the younger brother, Chad (AKA Breaker) in his journey, with his own set of weird powers, while Ex Gods follows the older, more jock/military brother, Drew. I might even have other 'future Elders' pop up in a new series eventually because it fits the model.

Where did this story come from? Originally, I was

considering doing a massive sort of LitMMO project, where it would be a more gamelit style than it is right now. I would bring in other authors to do other characters, while doing my story and a prequel to get things rolling. The problem is, I've managed projects like this before and they are a *huge* timesuck. Basically, instead of writing, I would have to be managing all of that. I'm a writer, not a project manager, so I decided to do most of it myself. I might have one other author do one—not as a ghost writer, but as himself—but otherwise, it's just me.

Oh, did you catch the woman at the beginning, with the golden glowing skull? Her story was going to be the prequel, and I even have a cover for it! Thing is, it wouldn't fit so smoothly into the genre of these other books, or with the brand of Jamie Hawke, so I'm still torn on that. If you think it would be cool to have a prequel from a female point of view—sort of a Spawn meets Deadpool type story—let me know! It could still happen.

Can I ask a favor? If you enjoyed this book, please go leave a review. Readers from the genre seemed to have enjoyed Ex Heroes 1, but when others who aren't familiar picked it up, they weren't sure what to think so reviews suffered. It would be great if all of you lovers of the genre could show your support via reviews. It's also a way to vote for what book you liked and which books should get sequels sooner. If it performs well and has great reviews, I'll know you all want more.

I also love hearing from you all! Find my Facebook group and join me in chatting about this story and others. What did you like most? What didn't work for you? Let's discuss.

Thank you again for reading!

Jamie Hawke

I'm super excited and hope you'll follow me on Facebook and Amazon (Click here and then 'Follow' under my name/pic). That way, you won't miss it! It's probably my best work ever.

Thank you again, and I look forward to hearing from you!

To connect directly:

https://www.facebook.com/groups/JamieHawke/

Also, for my GameLit Harem newsletter:

http://bit.ly/HaremGamelit

Do you want more Harem? I recommend this Facebook Group:

HaremGamelit Group

READ NEXT

Thank you for reading SUPERS: EX GODS! Please consider laving a review on Amazon and Goodreads. And don't miss out on the newsletter:

SIGN UP HERE

***

Don't miss the brother's story! If you are curious what happened to Drew's brother, Chad and want to check it out, read SUPERS: EX HEROES.

Super powers. Super harem. Super awesome.

Contains Adult Content. Seriously.

Who in their right mind tells both his lawyer and the judge presiding over his murder trial, "Fuck you!" while still in the courtroom? No one, right? Yeah, you'd be wrong about that. I did.

You'd say the same thing if you were just found guilty of a murder you didn't commit, though. Call me crazy for going off like that in court, but trust me, you don't know crazy until you see what happened next.

I never believed in superheroes. I certainly didn't believe that I'd become one, or that strategically forming a harem of hot chicas and getting down with them to unlock my superpowers would be the key to my survival.

Did I say my survival? I meant the universe's. No, really...that's exactly what happened when I was taken to a galaxy of supers, thrown into a prison ship full of villains, and told it was up to me to stop them all.

Read on, friend, because it gets a whole hell of a lot crazier from here.

***

Did you see the references to Planet Kill in the book and wonder what that was? It's not a real planet that I know of, but it is a real book! You can grab book one and two on Amazon!

Grab PLANET KILL now!

Form your harem. Kill or be killed. Level up and loot. Welcome to Planet Kill.

Pierce has his mission: survive by killing and getting nasty, doing whatever it takes to find his lost wife and others who were abducted and forced to participate in the barbarity that is Planet Kill. In a galaxy where the only way to rise up in society and make it to the paradise planets is through this insanity, he will be up against the most desperate, the most ruthless, and the sexiest fighters alive.

Because it's not just a planet--it's the highest rated show around. Contestants level up for kills, get paid for accepting violent and sexual bids, and factions have been made in the form of harems.

His plan starts to come together when he meets Letha, one of the most experienced warlords on the planet. She's as lethal as they come and a thousand times as sexy. He's able to learn under her, to start to form his own harem.

Only, being her ally means fighting her wars.

It's kill or be killed, level up fast and put on the show the viewers want all while proving to Letha and her generals that he has what it takes to be one of them. The alternative is death, leaving his wife to her fate of being hunted by monsters.

Grab book 2 - PLANET KILL: HAPPY HUNTING!

"They've taken Mortal Kombat meets Hunger Games and thrown a layer of debauchery on it. Brilliant!"

More blood, sex and death as one man fights against a deathly conspiracy—and one woman seeks justice.

He's forming his harem and is now a major player on Planet Kill. As Pierce makes his moves to cement his hold on power here, he continues his mission to escort forced volunteers off planet. Only, along the way he discovers a much broader conspiracy: one which threatens the nature of humanity.

She has her harem but is on the way up and out. She plans to ascend to Planet Paradise Fourteen, where she will finally have her revenge. If only this planet were everything it appeared to be on the surface, instead of the golden-framed and crystal-distorted mirror image of Planet Kill.

Guilty.

"Guilty?" I said, then turned to my lawyer, Jorge, unable to comprehend what was happening. "Did he just say guilty?"

Jorge leaned in and whispered, "Now, Chad… don't make it worse."

"Worse than guilty for murder?" I asked, my heart thudding in my ears. "Fuck you!" I turned to the judge, already wishing I wasn't saying the words as they left my mouth, but unable to stop it from happening, "And fuck you too!"

This wasn't happening. I wasn't standing here, shouting at a judge and my lawyer, cussing them out while the jury that had just decided my fate watched on. Only it was, and now those sons of bitches felt vindicated, more sure of their decision than ever simply because I used the words "Fuck" and "You." And because I was losing my shit.

Rightly so! Who the hell wouldn't if they were just found guilty of a murder they didn't commit?

Fuckheads with batons and guns had me, dragging me from court as I shouted, spittle spraying from my mouth. I think my arms were flailing, and I might've even hit one of them, and then I remembered something about the death sentence coming my way—or maybe it was life, I didn't care. Neither one of them was acceptable considering the fact that I was innocent.

The worst part? I knew the killer. Considering the fact that he was my brother, yeah, you could say I knew him quite well, though we'd drifted apart since he went off to the military. I'd been on my way back to the office when I saw Drew, ran over to ask what he was doing in town, and followed him into the bank.

I scanned the room and spotted him lunging into the path of some girl as a larger man shot some sort of blast her way. My only thought at the time was that my brother was being the typical hero, and was going to die for it. Only, then he'd stepped forward and slammed is hand into the man's chest, an act that had blasted the guy to bits. Or so we assumed, as there hadn't been a shred of the man left. There might have been a flash of light, an image of a woman reaching for Andrew before he vanished. It happened so fast, even I wasn't sure I believed that part.

There was no way I'd give him up in this, but it wasn't just loyalty. Sure, I'd have my eyeballs pulled out and replaced with my balls before giving him up, because he was blood. But my refusal to rat him out also had to do with the fact that they'd tell me I was insane.

Whatever had killed that other man, it hadn't been a simple gun or bomb or whatever they were trying to say I'd used. I saw that blast of energy come from my brother and nearly pissed myself—okay, there was a trickle of piss for sure—and then he was gone. My brother was gone!

One minute I was there, staring with a slack jaw and a bit of pee in my boxer-briefs, staring at my brother, and the next he was nowhere in sight and everyone was pointing at me, shouting, screaming, and it was chaos.

And it had all led to this moment. This horrible nightmare that had resulted in days of court, eye-witnesses pointing at me and saying I'd done it, and me having no argument except for the truth.

Truth, as it was clearly proven, didn't mean a damn thing.

If you've ever been sentenced to death, or life in prison, for a crime you didn't commit, you'll understand me when I say that what followed was all a blur. All I really remember was the hallway spinning, a pounding on the right side of my head, and multiple trips to the bathroom—mostly to vomit.

Really it was a like the feeling you get when someone takes a baseball bat to your nuts, and you know one of those testicles just died, never to return. Now imagine that but never stopping.

Well, then take the opposite of that. What's the opposite of that, you ask? I'll get there soon. Suffice it to say, I went from an extreme low to an extreme high very quickly.

My head cleared in the transport bus, me on my way to spend the rest of my life in prison. We were just turning down Central, an odor like burnt toast in the air, when shots sounded and the driver swerved.

I remember seeing a rocket launcher, and then recognizing a face from the truck next to us—Lenny, one of my adopted dad's associates, and then the explosions started. Best I could figure, this was my escape. Somehow, people involved with my dad were trying to break me out, which didn't make sense in any way, but when the bus went flying in the air, tipping over and about to slam me into the concrete, I knew they were failing.

Whoever was trying to break me free had just killed me.

And then it happened, the moment that would change me forever. When I say change, I mean FUCKING CHANGE.

Concrete was coming up fast, that damn smell of burnt toast growing stronger, and I noticed that my feet were asleep, or maybe I was having a stroke or something, because then it felt like my ass was asleep, a second later the side of my face.

Do asses fall asleep when you have a stroke? Hell, at the time I had no idea what was happening, but then the crash came… and blackness.

It wasn't death, I knew that much. There was too much pain for that to be the case. And yet, it wasn't the sort of pain you'd expect from a crash. It was like someone had pulled out my soul and then jammed it back inside me again.

At least the smell was gone, only now there was something in the air that made it feel sparse, a cold, staleness to it. My body was so cold.

When I looked around, I saw gray, metal walls. No windows. I was on the floor, and now I understood why I was cold—the floor was also metal, and I was nude. Completely nude! Lying on a metal floor without any clothes would do that.

Where the hell were my clothes?

(Keep Reading)

Made in the USA
Middletown, DE
30 October 2023

41647762R00189